# Cookies to
# **Die** For

# Cookies to **Die** For

*a novel of suspense*

## Dene Low

Covenant Communications, Inc.

Cover image: *Bullet Holes* © Caspar Benson, courtesy www.gettyimages.com/

Cover design copyright © 2014 by Covenant Communications, Inc.

Published by Covenant Communications, Inc.
American Fork, Utah

Printed in the United States of America
First Printing: May 2014

20 19 18 17 16 15 14     10 9 8 7 6 5 4 3 2 1

ISBN 978-1-62108-048-0

Dedicated to my awesome husband and to all my Relief Society sisters, who are indeed capable of overcoming absolutely anything.

World be warned.

# Acknowledgments

Thanks to my team at Covenant and the encouragement I've received from everyone who has read the manuscript. It is indeed a team effort to bring a book to publication: it requires not only the pros but family and friends who have to put up with crazy author stuff and crazy author mentality and love me anyway, almost as much as I love them.

# Prologue

I WAS SITTING IN MY writing class at the community college, listening. For somebody my age who hadn't been in school for more than twenty-five years, listening was hard work. I wasn't used to having to remember every word someone said to me. If one of my boys said, "Mom, I'm going over to Fred's house to look at his way cool new Honda Valkyrie. I'll be back about 10:00, so don't make dinner for me," I'd just hear, "Fred's house . . . 10:00 . . . don't make dinner." While he was telling me that, I'd be thinking about making cupcakes for his homeroom, calling my husband to tell him an order had finally come through at his auto parts store, and calculating liters of soda pop into gallons of punch for the Cub Scout social.

I'm just telling you that so you can picture how hard I had to concentrate while I was listening to Professor Mallory—so I wouldn't miss anything she was telling us about our final writing assignment. And because I was concentrating so much, what she said didn't really sink in until I'd repeated it to myself, so when I finally understood what she'd said, it hit me hard.

"I want you to write about what you know," she was telling us. "Write about a personal experience. So many of my students over the years have written improbable stories about spies or the CIA or the Mafia."

The class laughed.

"I always ask them, 'Do you know anyone who is a spy? Do you know any gangsters?'"

More laughter. I laughed along until I finished repeating the words to myself. Then I gasped. What she'd said wasn't funny. The whole reason I was taking this class was because I *did* know gangsters—only too well—and after the experiences I'd had with them, my therapist thought a writing class would be good for me, kind of a catharsis, and this was just the kind of assignment he'd hoped I'd get.

I went home that night from class and called Dr. Thornton, my therapist. He agreed that I should write about my experience with the gangsters, that it would be great therapy to get it down on paper. Then I could burn the manuscript or rip it to shreds or do something with it to show myself that episode was over and I could get on with my life.

As far as I was concerned, I was getting on with my life. Sometimes I thought Dr. Thornton was overly dramatic. The only reason I went to see him was to please Art, who'd learned about post-traumatic stress disorder while reading *Reader's Digest*. Sure, I'd gone through some pretty harrowing experiences. But then, what mother with four boys hadn't, and most didn't need post-traumatic stress therapy. Then again, some did. Still, I think Art wanted me to go to Dr. Thornton because my husband didn't know what else he could do for me. I suppose he felt the need to be involved in what had happened, even if it was only to pay for my therapist, especially since it was his fault I'd gotten involved with the gangsters in the first place. I think he kind of felt left out since I'd handled the whole thing by myself, but that was the way I'd wanted it. I'd done everything in my power to keep those gangsters away from my family.

# Chapter One

IT WASN'T EXACTLY A DARK and rainy night. In fact, it was only a little overcast and rather cool for the season. However, I'm still going to start with just as trite a beginning statement.

*NOTE: I know, Professor Mallory, you warned us against being trite. I understand that, according to you, being trite is second only to shedding innocent blood. But I can't think of any other way to start.*

It all began last spring with Memorial Day weekend. Art had taken the boys and the dog on a week-long camping trip to celebrate the end of school, especially since Brant had actually stayed in school the entire year, which was a huge victory for him. I was happy for him and for me. Nobody likes getting calls from the neighbors that their son is hanging out in the park instead of in school. I was ecstatically looking forward to a whole week with nothing to do other than check in on Art's auto shop, which he'd named Art's Parts (he has a weird sense of humor), to make sure the assistant manager was keeping things running smoothly.

For nearly seven days, I was going to eat when I wanted and what I wanted, take showers without someone turning on the washing machine or dishwasher and either scalding or freezing me, get up when I wanted to, and sleep when I wanted to. I knew that, by the end of the week, I was going to be missing Art and the boys something awful, but I intended to enjoy myself as long as I could. Then when I started missing them, I was going to start baking all of their favorite things to have waiting for them when they came home. I am a great cook, with the hips to prove it. I only mention cooking and hips because they are part of the story, what Professor Mallory calls foreshadowing. What I didn't know was that those seven days were going to be the worst week I'd ever lived, except for the weeks after Art's accident. More about that later.

I was humming as I went around to the back of the mini-van to get the groceries. That evening I'd been to a Cub Scout dinner and then to the grocery store to stock up for the coming week so I wouldn't have to go shopping again until my family came home. On my way around the minivan, I saw a flashlight on Art's workbench, which reminded me that the brakes had been acting funny all evening. I'd tried to look at them in the parking lot of the supermarket, but it had been too dark. With the garage light and the flashlight, maybe I could get a better look.

I put a rag on the garage floor and carefully kneeled on the cloth so that I wouldn't get my dark blue Cub Scout pants dirty; I was also careful not to touch the minivan with my yellow Scout shirt as I shined the flashlight on the brakes. I blinked. That couldn't be what I thought it was. Puzzled,

I leaned closer for a better look. I was right. There was a rope tied to the brakes. It wasn't tied in a place to do any real harm, but if the responsible party had tied it elsewhere, I could have been killed. Was this someone's idea of a joke? If so, it was a stupid one. I could feel a slow burn building, only to be quickly doused by a second thought. If it wasn't a joke, then someone was serious about hurting me. Why would anyone want to hurt or even kill me?

I decided I'd better call the police, which, for me, was synonymous with Manny Ruiz. Manny lived two houses away and was a policeman on the Colorado Springs police force. He and his family joined the Church three years ago, after Art had invited them over for family home evening, our one and only success as member missionaries and one I was really pleased with. The Ruizes are great people who had enthusiastically changed their lifestyles to fit with the gospel. Now Manny was a counselor in the elders quorum and his wife, Angela, was a Primary teacher. They said they owed us a lot for introducing the gospel to them, but we owed them a lot too. As a friend and our home teacher, Manny had been a big help when our son Brant had gone rebellious and wild, so it was natural for me to call Manny for help when Art was gone.

*NOTE: Professor Mallory, I know you might not understand all the references to church things, but they're an important part of the story, so if you want an explanation, just ask me. I'll be happy to tell you anything you want to know about the LDS Church.*

After gathering my purse and the two grocery sacks containing refrigerated food, I went into the kitchen, thinking about whether I should call or just run over to the Ruiz's since they lived so close. Calling won. For one thing, it was late and they were probably getting ready for bed. For another, as frightened as I was, running through the dark night where all kinds of scary villains might be lurking just didn't appeal to me. I preferred the "safety" of my own home.

I deposited the food in the refrigerator then went to the phone. That's when I experienced one of those nightmare moments when I suddenly knew someone was behind me. I didn't hear anyone. I didn't even feel any kind of movement. Yet I knew someone was there.

If I'd been frightened before, what I felt next could only be classified as cold, panicked terror. My hand shot toward the phone receiver only to feel a strong man grip my wrist like an iron vise. I screamed. It was a large hand with black hair on the back. No one in my family had black hair or hairy hands. I screamed again.

I need to pause to explain my behavior so you won't think I'm a violent person: Of my four boys, the two oldest, Kyle and Evan, had played football in high school. No matter how often I'd told them how fragile their mother was, they always seemed to think of me as their personal tackle dummy, and I usually had the bruises to show for it. Out of sheer desperation, I'd paid particular attention to Manny when he'd demonstrated self-defense maneuvers at a weeknight Relief Society meeting. While I wasn't exactly a black belt in karate, I'd learned enough to keep myself from being pulverized and at least make Kyle and Evan think twice about attacking me. I'd never been vicious with them, just firm.

However, as soon as that hand clamped over my mouth, I automatically went into defense mode, and panic lent me a viciousness usually foreign to my calm personality.

I twisted in the man's grasp, using the force of my whole body to drive my elbow into his stomach. At the same time, I stomped as hard as I could on whatever I could connect with—his foot—two, three times. He let out an "Oof" when my elbow hit and a couple of grunts when I smashed his foot. I felt his grip weaken on my arm and mouth, so I brought my free hand up, grabbed his little finger on the hand across my mouth, and twisted the pinky sharply. There was a crack, and he yelled. Manny had said this was the best way for a weaker person to make a stronger person let go. Manny was right. The man let go, and I squirmed away.

I would have gotten clean away too, if it hadn't been for the other guy.

As I raced around the kitchen into the living room, a strong pair of arms grabbed me around the waist and lifted me, kicking and struggling. Containing me was no mean feat since I'm rather chubby, but then, he was pretty big. Whoever it was carried me back through the kitchen into the family room and plopped me into the reclining chair. He held me there by my shoulders, pushing the chair back so I was lying down. The first man yanked an extension cord out of the wall socket, not caring when the attached lamp came crashing down, and tied me into the chair with the cord, jerking it tight enough to bite into my arms. He must have been infuriated with me for breaking his finger, so pulling that cord tight was his way of getting even. He certainly cussed enough every time he had to move his hand. When he was through, he stepped back, staring malevolently at me like I was a trussed-up pig ready for slaughter.

For the first time, I got a good look at the two men. The one with the broken finger was medium height and had neatly trimmed black hair and a beard. He was probably in his early thirties. He didn't look like a criminal. Neither did his clothes look like what I supposed a criminal would wear—blue jeans, Nike Air shoes, and a polo shirt. At the moment, he was nursing his finger. I decided I was fortunate to have broken his finger instead of the other guy's—that one looked mean. Actually, he looked kind of like Brant a year ago—shaved head, bandana, earrings, black leather, and chains from neck to toe. The man seemed older than Brant, maybe in his early twenties. Scary. I remember when Brant showed up for my birthday party last year looking like this guy's younger brother. I thought, as he'd given me a hug, that if I hadn't raised him from a baby, there was no way I'd let someone who looked like that anywhere near me. Now I didn't have a choice.

"No more screaming," instructed Beard through gritted teeth. "No more, or I'll let the kid here gag you, and he enjoys that kind of thing. OK?"

The kid briefly tightened his fingers hard on my shoulders. There'd be bruises tomorrow.

I nodded. I doubted whether my screams would have done any good anyway. The neighbors on either side weren't very friendly. In fact, the couple in the house between us and the Ruiz's was downright antagonistic about how many children we had, probably because they didn't have any themselves. Once they'd even called the police on Kyle and Evan for "disturbing the peace" when all the boys had been doing was having an early-morning football practice in our backyard. After that, the neighbors had built an eight-foot fence between our yards. The couple would probably jump for joy if they knew I was in trouble.

Besides, I didn't know if I *could* scream anymore. My throat seemed to have tightened up to the point I was having trouble getting enough air. I could feel my heart thumping at breakneck speed and perspiration gathering at my temples. I had to deliberately calm myself so I didn't pass out. I knew that to do so would be disastrous. I needed my wits about me to assess the situation. Obviously, physical prowess was not going to do me any good. There was no way I was even going to be able to get out of the chair, especially while they were watching me. I needed to think. I needed to know why these men were here and what they wanted, but I didn't want to anger them any more than I already had. I especially didn't want to get hurt. It's a funny thing, but enduring pain inflicted because of hate or anger is not as easy as enduring pain because of illness or accident. I was at their mercy, and I was afraid of what they might do.

My gaze traveled around the room for some clue about what they'd been doing in my house. My eyes passed over the couch—the upholstery ripped and the stuffing spilling out—and rested on the open file-cabinet drawer next to Art's desk. Then I noticed the desk drawers were pulled partially open as well. The only things in those drawers had to do with Art's auto parts store. Did this have to do with Art's business? Was Art in trouble? Was the rope on the brakes meant for Art and not me? Art had been using the van lately while he was waiting for a part to come in for his truck.

Suddenly, the panic in me focused into a hard, sharp point. I forgot about my own safety and could only think about protecting my husband. I was glad he wasn't here. I couldn't bear for anything to happen to him—especially after what we'd gone through after his accident. I was glad my children weren't here either. I didn't know what I'd do if they were threatened. The thought made me go all quivery inside. Somehow I had to get rid of these men, and that came back to finding out what they wanted. *Please,* I prayed, *please help me protect my family.*

# Chapter Two

I FORCED MY THROAT OPEN, allowing enough air to pass through to ask, "Why are you here?"

They didn't answer. Beard flopped onto the couch and looked at me through narrowed eyes, while Kid grabbed Art's desk chair and sat on it backward so he could rest his chin on the high back. He had picked up a knife from the floor—one of those long ornamentally curved things with silver insets in the black handle—and was running his index finger over it. It looked sharp. I hoped he'd cut himself on it. When he saw me looking at him, he flicked the knife in my direction, grinning evilly when I jumped. He glanced from me to Beard and back again, as if waiting for the older man to respond. Beard was gingerly running the index finger from his good hand along his broken finger. It must have hurt.

A glimmer of an idea broke through. It was only a tiny glimmer, but it gave me hope. I remembered a story Marietta Heinrich, our Relief Society compassionate service teacher, had told recently about the Prophet Joseph Smith and how he'd escaped jail once because he'd made friends with his jailer. I didn't know how I was going to get these hoodlums to let me loose from this chair, but that finger looked like my first opportunity to gain some trust.

"Where's your computer?" Beard asked.

Startled, I blinked. That wasn't at all what I'd expected him to say. "Where are your jewels?" would have been more like it. Then again, I'm not the jewelry type, and he probably saw that in an instant. I whispered, "We don't have a computer."

Beard cussed. He punched his fist into the palm of his hand and cussed again, evidently because of the pain from his broken finger—at least, he waved it around like it hurt.

*NOTE: Professor Mallory, I know you've told us to connect with reality in our writing, but I simply cannot and will not use garbage-can words, even if the characters really did use them. So when I say someone cussed or swore, you know that what they said was simply terrible.*

As Beard cussed and waved his hand around, my glimmer of hope brightened. I gulped before saying, "I can fix that."

Beard stopped in mid-wave and glared at me. "Fix what? That you don't have a computer?" Kid laughed like it was a very funny joke until Beard transferred his glare to him.

I gulped again. "I can fix your finger so it doesn't hurt so much." My voice sounded weak.

"You can what?" He glared at me again. I could see he was thinking that I was the one who had made his finger hurt in the first place, so what was I doing offering to fix it?

"I can fix your finger so it doesn't hurt so much," I repeated.

He didn't say anything, just looked at me thoughtfully until I was ready to either scream or laugh hysterically. Of course, I did neither. He got up from the couch and leaned over me. As he untied the cord, he growled, "Don't try anything."

I shook my head. The relief from the pressure was enormous. I hadn't realized just how tight the cord had been until it was released. I definitely didn't want to be tied up again. By the next day, I'd not only have Kid's finger marks on my shoulders, I'd have cord marks on my arms and body. But I wasn't about to complain, even if I was in pain. Shakily, I raised the chair to a sitting position and stood. Motioning toward the bathroom, I said, "The stuff to fix your finger is in there."

Beard nodded. He followed me, watching as I opened the cupboard under the sink and pulled out two plastic bins. The first contained lots of elastic bandages. I chose a narrow one then rooted around in the second bin until I found the right kind of finger splint. I glanced up at Beard and explained, "I have sons who play football. I'm Red Cross certified in first aid." I hoped my Cub Scout uniform would make him believe me.

"If you're going to get your finger broke, you ought to at least get it broke by someone who knows how to fix it," said Kid over Beard's shoulder. He laughed even louder than when he'd laughed at Beard. Kid had an obnoxious laugh—nasal and high, with a machine gun, repetitive "heh, heh, heh, heh." From the look on Beard's face, that noise made him want to punch Kid in the nose. Interesting. They didn't like each other. Maybe their dislike of each other would be a good thing for me. Who'd said, "Divide and conquer?" I knew it wasn't a quote from the Book of Mormon, though Captain Moroni had used that tactic, but it might be good advice anyway.

"Let's go in the kitchen, where the light is better," I said. They followed me into the kitchen without protest. My flame of hope burned even brighter as I felt a shift of power in my direction—just a little shift, but a shift nonetheless. Confidence crept back into my soul. Feeling better, I sat Beard in a chair at my kitchen table and deftly bandaged his finger. There's something about a mother in her own kitchen that is irrefutably powerful. I sensed it, and I could tell these two men sensed it as well, although they might not have understood it. All the better for me if they didn't. I decided to stay in the kitchen as much as possible—on my turf.

"There," I said as I attached the fastener to the elastic bandage I'd wound around Beard's finger, hand, and wrist. "That should feel much better."

Beard held his bandaged hand out in front of him, turning it from side to side as if examining my handiwork. It was quite professional looking, if I do say so myself. But then, I'd had a lot of practice. I could tell Beard was pleased and that the bandage helped relieve his pain because the tightness around his eyes had relaxed, just like Art's eyes had when he had felt relief from pain after his accident.

"Where's your husband?" he asked without warning.

Any confidence I'd felt drained out of me. Just having that man's slimy lips mention my husband was like a desecration—a violation of what was good and pure and most dear to me. Then I realized that Art was out of reach. I couldn't tell where he was because I didn't know where he was. Art and the boys had planned on doing some exploring. They were backpacking into a wilderness area where no one would be able to find them. Keeping my eyes down so Beard couldn't see the relief in them, I said, "I don't know. He and the boys went camping somewhere and won't be back for a week."

The door to the garage opened. Both Beard and I glanced up sharply. I hadn't seen Kid leave and I guess neither had the older man, but there he was with both arms loaded with groceries. He announced, "She's got enough food to feed an army. Look at all of this, and there's still more out there—besides all the stuff she already put in the fridge." He set the sacks on the counter next to the ones I'd already emptied.

"Why did you buy so much food if your family's gone?" accused Beard.

"I didn't want to have to go shopping again until they got home." It was a good thing I could tell the truth, since it's much more convincing than a lie. But I was prepared to lie through my teeth if it meant protecting my family. In fact, I was praying with all my might that God would help me come up with the most convincing whoppers of all time if it was necessary.

"You lie!" Beard stared hard at me through narrowed eyes.

Caught off guard by the irony of his accusation, I had to bite my tongue to keep from laughing in his face. I said as innocently as I could, "Really, it's the truth. Why would I lie about a thing like that?"

"So we'd go away." Beard flung open the refrigerator door, causing the salad dressing bottles to dance in the door shelves. "Just look at this food. All of this won't keep for a whole week." He grabbed a quart of Häagen-Dazs ice cream off the top shelf, shaking it in my face. "And what about this. It looks like you were keeping it soft, ready to serve. There's enough here for a whole family."

Heat rushed up my neck. The ice cream was meant for me—all of it—but I wasn't about to admit that. I was planning on eating the whole carton while I watched *A Guy*

*Named Joe* after I'd put the groceries away. My whole family hates that movie, but I love it because it's the only sappy romance I know of where the girl actually saves the guy's life. I was going to get into my jammies, wrap a quilt around me, watch the movie, and eat the whole entire quart of ice cream. There was another quart in the freezer for the next night—and the next and the next, etc.

Mustering as much dignity as I could under the circumstances, I said, "What I told you is the truth. They won't be back for a week. I was planning on cooking most of the food so it would be ready for them when they get back."

Beard took a deep breath, as if his patience was almost at an end. "I don't believe you."

"What are we going to tell the boss if this guy doesn't show tonight?" asked Kid.

"He'll show," said Beard.

As if losing interest, Kid started rummaging around in the refrigerator. "Well, it might end up being a long wait, and I'm starved." He straightened and looked at me. "Hey! What were you going to cook for your old man?"

My initial reaction was to resent Kid's eating any of my food, but then I realized that this was my ticket to staying in the kitchen and moving around freely instead of being tied up. Besides, hadn't Brigham Young told the pioneers to feed the Indians instead of making them enemies? I answered, "Pot roast, chicken Parmesan, lasagna, twice-baked potatoes, broccoli in cheese sauce, potatoes au gratin, apple pie, cheesecake, chocolate chip cookies, chocolate cake . . ."

A big grin spread across Kid's face. "What's fastest, the pot roast or the chicken Parmesan?"

"Pot roast, if I use the pressure cooker," I said.

Kid turned to Beard. "What about it? You want a pot roast dinner?"

Beard shook his head as if disgusted by the whole conversation. "Whatever. It'll keep her out of trouble. But you have to watch her." He went into the family room and turned on the TV.

"Let's go for the pot roast dinner," said Kid. "But first make me a big pot of coffee."

I froze. Then as calmly as I could, I said, "I don't have any coffee. We don't drink it."

"You've got to be kidding! No coffee? Give me a break!"

I shook my head. "No. You can look, if you like."

Disgusted, Kid grabbed my Häagen-Dazs and plunked himself down into a kitchen chair where he could see the TV. "Just hurry up with the pot roast then. I'll make do with this," he said and dug into the ice cream with every indication that he was planning to enjoy himself.

Sighing over the loss of my ice cream, I got out the roast and started it browning in the pressure cooker; then I went to work on the potatoes and carrots. I supposed I should be grateful Kid hadn't gotten violent because I didn't have coffee. I could just see him slitting my throat with that knife. My stomach was tied up in knots. I was in mid-slice when Beard came back into the kitchen and laid a revolver on the table in front of Kid. My stomach tightened further as Beard said, "She's using knives. Shoot her if she gets any ideas." He looked at me looking at him. "She'd be hard to miss."

That was low. I wasn't hugely obese, just pudgy. In some way, his remark released the tightness in my stomach. Turning back to the potatoes, I whipped the skin off the next one in record time. Hard to miss, my eye.

"Pow!"

I jumped, nearly cutting my hand.

"Pow! Pow!" Kid was pointing the gun at me, pretending to shoot. When he saw that he'd startled me, he laughed his

machine-gun laugh. If he had been one of my kids, I would
have thrown the potatoes at him. But that gun was real, and
if his laugh was anything to go by, he was as unbalanced as
the Leaning Tower of Pisa. We locked eyes. Squinting along
the revolver barrel one more time, he clicked his tongue as
if releasing the hammer. Then he laid it on the table again
next to his knife. He went back to the Häagen-Dazs, and I
went back to the potatoes and carrots, consciously slowing my
breathing as I peeled and sliced until I felt my heart rate was
nearly back to normal.

"While the pot roast is cooking, you can make chocolate
chip cookies. Do you know how to make those big ones?"
Kid asked.

I dumped carrots and potatoes into the pressure cooker
with the now-browned roast. "Yes, I was planning on making
some of the big ones with chunks of chocolate instead of
chocolate chips, but I have chips too. Which do you like
best?" I asked as I poured water over the contents of the
pressure cooker then added the spices.

"The big chunks of chocolate," he said, grinning again.
If it hadn't been for his earrings, bandana, black leather,
knife, and chains, he would have looked like a five-year-old
thinking about Christmas morning.

By the time the pressure cooker was spitting steam, I was
creaming the shortening and sugar for the cookies. Because
the spitting cooker and the sound of the mixer made such a
huge amount of noise, it wasn't until the answering machine
clicked on that I realized the telephone had been ringing.
Turning the mixer off, I automatically went to answer the
phone, but as I lifted the receiver, Kid grabbed me from
behind, one hand going over my mouth. As someone famous
once said, it was déjà vu all over again. I dropped the phone,

reached for Kid's little finger, and yanked. It cracked. He yelled. Beard bounded into the kitchen, replaced the phone receiver, and slapped my face.

For a moment it was like we were in a still photograph, me with my hand to my stinging cheek, eyes wide, staring at Beard. Kid was doubled over his injured hand. Beard was pointing his finger in my face.

The phone rang again. One. Two. Three. Four. Beard and I didn't move, but Kid sank into a kitchen chair, groaning and clutching his finger. Then he grabbed his knife and dove for me. He would have had me too, except Beard grabbed him from behind with an arm around Kid's neck. "Kill her before we get what we need and the boss will kill you," Beard growled through gritted teeth. Kid glared at me, his eyes slitted, but Beard's threat must have carried some weight because he relaxed. Beard let him go to sit on the chair and nurse his hurt finger. I just stood there shaking, unable to move.

The answering machine clicked on. When the machine had beeped, Kyle's voice said, "All right, Brant. Cut the funny stuff and answer the phone." Pause. "Mom? Are you there? Is anyone there?" Pause. "Oh, well. I just called to let you know we're coming through Colorado Springs on our way to Seattle for Veronica's brother's high school graduation. We hope to be to your house by Tuesday, and if it's all right with you, we'd like to stay a couple of days before making the rest of the trip. Then on the way back we'd like to stay a week. This driving from Houston is the pits, but we can't afford the plane fare. Hope you still love us when you see us. By then the kids will be out of control. See you in a few days. Sure do love you." Then he hung up.

While Kyle spoke, my gaze had left Beard's face and focused on a family portrait on the wall. It had been taken when Kyle and Veronica's youngest was only a few months old. Now little Casey was nearly two, and I hadn't seen her or any of her family for over a year. My heart leaped at the thought of seeing them again on Tuesday, along with the rest of her family. I thought, *Won't they be surprised to find out what had happened to good ol' stay-at-home Mom.* I just hoped they wouldn't walk into the middle of it. My heart rate went up at the thought of these gangsters meeting up with my darlings. There was no way I was going to let that happen, but what was I going to do?

"Fix his finger," snapped Beard.

Without answering, I went to get the bandages, with Beard right behind me. Before Kyle and his family got here, I'd have to somehow get rid of Kid and Beard. *Please,* I prayed, *please help me find a way to get rid of these criminals. Please help me keep my family safe.*

# Chapter Three

SLEEPING WHILE SITTING UP HAS never been a favorite pastime of mine, although I've done it more times than I can remember when my family has been sick. The worst was during the days and nights Art was in the hospital after his accident—I sat up night after night next to his bed, his still hand clutched in mind as I fearfully watched every fluctuation of his blood pressure, pulse, and oxygen level until I was exhausted. Sometimes I would wake with a start only to find my cheek planted against Art's arm and my back aching, but I wasn't about to let go of Art's hand. I knew he could tell I was there, even if he was unconscious.

One night a nurse took pity on me and wheeled a gurney in next to Art's bed so I could lie down while holding his hand. The next morning, I woke when the sun shone in my eyes. When I turned to look at Art, I saw he was conscious for the first time since they'd brought him into the hospital. The sun made his eyes very blue. I just stared at them. I'd never seen anything so beautiful in my life. Art was intubated, so he couldn't talk, but he weakly raised the hand I wasn't holding and brushed it across his face in the sign language motion for *beautiful.* I realized he thought I was beautiful too. I'm afraid I kissed him, tubes and all. Later he told me that kissing while intubated was not at all stimulating, but he appreciated the gesture.

I woke the morning after being captured, half thinking I was back in the hospital. I was disappointed to find that Beard and Kid were still there and that the crick in my back was from slumping over the kitchen table. Instead of sun in my eyes, there was just the sound of rain on the roof and no Art to hold my hand. I was alone with two thugs. I had to remind myself that that was the way I wanted it, as long as the thugs were around. As soon as I got rid of them, I wanted to throw myself into Art's arms and just feel safe, but not until then.

Cautiously, I stretched. Beard's head swung in my direction. He got up from the easy chair where he'd been watching the morning news and came into the kitchen.

"Where's your husband camping?" he asked.

I was surprised by the question. The night before, he certainly hadn't believed me when I'd told him Art and the boys had gone camping. Evidently the fact that they hadn't come home had convinced him. "I don't know. He didn't say."

Beard's hand closed over the gun. He said through gritted teeth, "He must have told you something in case of emergency."

I shrugged, relieved I couldn't tell the man what he wanted to hear. From the look on his face, he probably would have enjoyed slapping me again. I hurried to add, "He wanted some time alone with his boys, no interruptions. He said that nothing short of the Second Coming would make him come home early."

"The Second what?" asked Beard.

"The end of the world," I explained, which wasn't entirely truthful but close enough. He didn't appear to be listening anyway. He just sat there staring at the gun, flicking the little safety catch with the nail of his index finger. At least the thing wasn't pointed at me. I didn't know which was worse, Beard's gun or Kid's knife.

The channels on the TV changed several times, finally stopping on a TV evangelist. Out of the corner of my eye, I saw the top of Kid's head rise above the back of the couch, so he was awake. Too bad. I was hoping he'd be like Brant and sleep most of the day. It was easier dealing with one at a time. Then again, if they talked to each other, maybe I could figure out what was going on.

Kid heaved himself off the torn-up couch and stumbled into the kitchen, scratching first the stubble on his chin and then the stubble on his head. Brant had said the worst part of having a shaved head was the way it itched when it needed shaving. I had answered in all sincerity that keeping up an image required a certain amount of sacrifice—no pain no gain. He had just given me one of those "Oh, Mom" looks. I love "Oh, Mom" looks. They make up so nicely for the sacrifice I made giving the child the breath of life.

"I'm going to take a shower. I want pancakes and bacon ready when I come out," Kid said to me before turning to head for the bathroom. He held the knife point under my nose just long enough to make me close my eyes and shudder. This was a little game he'd played several times the night before, and I'd decided to give him the reaction he wanted, since he stopped tormenting me when I did.

"You've got to be kidding. You can't be hungry after all that stuff you ate last night," said Beard, indicating the piles of dishes I'd washed in the wee hours of the morning.

Kid turned on his heel to face us. "Me! You ate your share too. I didn't finish a whole pot roast off by myself, or the cookies, or the two pies and the cake!"

*But he had eaten my Häagen-Dazs ice cream,* I thought, *the whole quart.*

Beard shifted in his chair so he didn't have to look at the younger man. "I don't know why I even bother talking to you."

"Because you're worried about what I'll say to the boss when I call him and report you haven't found what he sent you to find." Kid spat on the carpet. I made a note of where so I could sterilize it when he left. He hooked his fingers through his belt loops and sneered, "You think you're such a big man." He raised his voice in mocking mimicry. "Send me, boss. I bet I know right where it is, boss." He lowered his voice. "But it wasn't right where you thought it was. In fact, there isn't even the slightest clue in this place about where it might be. The boss was right to send me along to keep an eye on you."

Beard slammed his good hand onto the table as he rose from his chair. "The boss never sent you to be my watchdog! You're in this every bit as much as I am. More, even. I leased out the office suite on the boss's orders, but you were the one who sold everything off without checking with anyone. If anything, the boss is giving you a second chance by sending you on this assignment. That's why I'm in charge and you're not!"

Beard stepped away from the table toward Kid, and Kid took a step toward Beard. Their faces were grim and antagonistic. Kid especially looked frightening—scarier than

Brant ever had—as if he could kill. If it had been Kyle and Evan facing off, I would have been apprehensive enough, expecting a major battle any second, but this confrontation was potentially more dangerous, especially with a gun and knife around.

The gun! It was on the table, and Beard was farther away from it than I was. He wasn't paying any attention to it either—or to me. His entire focus was on Kid, fist clenched around the knife, waving it menacingly. And Kid's entire focus was on Beard. Holding my breath, I inched my hand across the table. Closer. Closer. I didn't want to make any sudden movements. I prayed they wouldn't notice me. Closer. Just as I felt the tips of my fingers brush against cold steel, Beard lunged sideways, scooped up the gun, and pointed it at Kid.

Once again it was as if we were frozen in a photograph—Kid's arm stiff in front of him, Beard's arm stiff out in front of him, me sitting stiffly at the table.

After several seconds, Beard growled, "Go take your shower. And make it cold."

I watched Kid's fingers clench and unclench around the knife. So did mine—on nothing. More's the pity. Then Kid let out his breath, turned on his heel, and stalked into the bathroom. Right then he reminded me even more of Brant, especially the stiff shoulders. It was only after Kid slammed the door that I realized I needed air and took a shuddering breath.

Beard sat down at the kitchen table with apparent calm. He placed the gun on the table in front of him and wiped his hands, staring at the gun. I stared too. He glanced up. Our eyes met. Stiffening, he snapped, "You better make breakfast, like he said."

By the time Kid came out of the bathroom, the bacon was sizzling and I'd started the pancakes cooking. As he sat down opposite Beard, Kid sniffed appreciatively, grinning. "Now don't that smell good," he said, his good humor apparently restored. Showers can do that, and so can the smell of bacon. Don't ask me why. I think it has something to do with negative ions. I'll have to ask Dr. Thornton.

As I set plates full of steaming food in front of each of them, I noticed Kid's now smooth head and face. I wondered whose razor he'd used. Probably mine. I'd have to get a new one.

Kid waved his hand in front of my face. "I took the bandage off to take a shower. Rewrap it." He laid the knife on the table in front of him as if daring me to make a wrong move.

While I was obediently taking care of the finger, the phone rang. Beard stared at me, warning me with his eyes not to move toward the phone. After the fourth ring and Art's cheerful instructions about leaving a message, Mary Ann Griffith said, "Hi, Jane. This is Mary Ann. It's the last Sunday of the month, so you know what that means. Is it all right if Carline and I come over after church? I'll see you in Relief Society and you can tell me. OK? Bye!"

I blinked. That's right. It was Sunday morning. Glancing at the clock, I saw it was just after nine. Church was at eleven.

"Who are Mary Ann and Carline?" Beard asked.

"Friends," I answered, unwilling to explain the whole visiting teaching program. It would kind of be casting pearls before swine.

*NOTE: That doesn't mean I wouldn't explain it to you, Professor Mallory. Like I said, I'll be happy to explain anything you don't understand about church stuff.*

"So what does it mean about the last Sunday of the month?" Beard sounded suspicious.

"We usually get together once a month, and so far, we haven't yet. This is the last time we could see each other before the end of the month," I said, hoping that would satisfy him.

"Hm," he said.

Before he could say anything else, I asked, "May I go in the bathroom?" They'd let me go once the night before, so I was pretty sure the answer would be yes. Besides being important to my physical well-being, I wanted to establish a pattern of going into the bathroom regularly because I was starting to formulate a plan.

Beard shrugged. "Go ahead. Just remember I can see the door from here."

He didn't know it, but that was exactly what I wanted him to say. I was on my way into the bathroom when the phone rang again. I paused to hear who it was. "Hello, this is Manny, your late home teacher. I know I said we'd get there early this month, but you know how things are. Would it be okay if we came by this evening about seven? There are only four more days in the month, and I have to work tomorrow night because it's Memorial Day. Call me back, or talk to me at church. See you."

"More friends?" Beard said sarcastically.

I just nodded and slipped into the bathroom. I really did need to go. When I was finished, I turned on the water in the sink as hard as it would go to drown out any noises I made as I checked things out—like the window, which was over the bathtub. Stepping into the bathtub, I realized the window was higher than I'd thought. I could reach the latch, but the sill was about even with my nose, which was great when I showered but not when I was trying to climb out of it. I

climbed up onto the edge of the bathtub and used the inset
soap dish on the other side for one foot to rest on. Straddling
the tub, I was able to reach the window and slide it open.
Just looking at that narrow opening, I could tell I'd never get
through, even if I could get up there. I could get the sliding
part of the window out of the track and take off the screen.
That would give me another inch. I might make it then, but
it would be a tight squeeze. Not for the first time, I cursed
the size of my hips.

As I leaned forward to lift the window out of its track, my
foot slipped from the soap dish. I teetered on the edge of the
tub, my arms waving frantically until I grabbed the shower
curtain, still wet from Kid's shower. That steadied me for a
moment, but my weight must have been too much for the
rod because it started to come down on my head. I grabbed
it just in time, before it clattered against anything. I rested on
the edge of the bathtub with my eyes closed, hugging the wet
shower curtain, hanging onto the loose curtain rod, and giving
thanks that I hadn't made any noise. Carefully, I stepped down
onto the floor, making sure I didn't hit anything with that rod.
Then I reattached the rod where it had left marks on the wall.
Luckily it was one of those expandable rods that didn't need
any hardware, so it went back up easily enough. A glance at
my watch showed me I'd been in the bathroom about ten minutes. Five minutes too long. I wasn't going to be able to carry
out my plan right then. They were probably wondering what I
was doing and would be checking up on me any minute.

In less than thirty seconds, I had closed the window and
fixed my makeup and hair so it at least looked like that was
what had taken me so long, although I could scarcely stand to
look at myself in the mirror. My yellow and blue Cub Scout
uniform was crumpled and damp from the shower curtain,
and I had black circles under my eyes. I looked terrible. Not

even the makeup helped. When I was finished, I took a deep breath and went back to the kitchen.

The first thing I noticed was that Beard was rifling through Art's filing cabinet. What was it he wanted? He was in the drawer with all of our tax files.

"Hey, you. Old lady," said Kid, pulling his head out of the refrigerator and shutting the door.

"Yes?" I turned to face him, my stomach tightening at the thought of facing that knife again. Normally, the way he was talking to me would have made me angry, but right then I wanted him to think of me as old and frail and unable to climb out of windows, even if I had broken his finger.

"How about starting some lasagna. That takes a long time, doesn't it? You have some cake mixes too. I want the lemon one, with homemade lemon icing. None of that fake stuff in a can. And then—"

"You're not going to have time to eat all of that," interrupted Beard, coming from the family room with some papers in his hand. For the first time since this ordeal had begun, he was smiling. His eyes never left my face as he walked over to the answering machine and triumphantly punched the replay button. I stood transfixed as I listened.

"Jane, this is George. Did Manny get hold of you about tonight? I forgot to tell him Art and the boys were planning on going camping this week—where was it Art said? Near Florrisant, wasn't it? Great home teaching companion I am. Anyway, I guess we won't catch the whole family tonight, but at least we can come see you. I'll talk to you at church, and you can tell me if tonight's OK. See you."

As the machine clicked off, Beard pointed his index finger at me, punching the air in front of him. "Your husband is camping somewhere near Florrisant. You lied when you said you didn't know where he was."

I shrugged. "He never told me he was going to Florrisant." Which was true. Art had said he really hadn't made up his mind about which way he was going. I didn't have a clue about why he'd mentioned Florrisant to George.

Beard continued, "After that guy called, I got the idea to look in your files for this." He waved the paper-clipped papers in my face, and I got a glimpse of a car title and insurance papers. "Here's the description of your husband's truck and his license plate number. I'm sending the kid here up to the campgrounds near Florrisant with this information to find your husband and sons."

It was all I could do to keep my face emotionless when all I wanted more than anything to scratch the scum's eyes out of his smug face and strangle him at the same time. I was shocked by the intense desire to inflict pain that rose up inside me when he threatened my family, but I managed to fix my gaze on the floor, willing myself not to react to Beard's taunting. In a flat voice, I said, "There's a lot of territory around Florrisant."

Beard chuckled. "But not that many places to camp overnight, and a lot less if it's still under snow, especially with the rain we're getting. If it's raining down here, it could be snowing up there. It won't take the kid more than a few hours to find a truck like this." He held up the papers and read, "Ford F150 pickup, purple, with a license that says RTSPRTS. I don't see how he can miss it."

I'd told Art not to get vanity plates or paint his truck purple, but he'd thought it would be great advertising. For once I was sorry I had the chance to say I told you so.

"What if I don't want to go? Who wants to get all wet in the rain and snow?" said Kid.

Beard's face hardened. "You don't have any choice. It's almost time to call the boss. Do you want me to tell him you refuse to follow the only real lead we have, or do you want to be off doing something he'll be happy about?" Beard sneered.

Kid's eyes narrowed. He angrily pushed a kitchen chair out of his way as he stormed into the family room and grabbed his leather jacket, heavy with clanking silver chains. Before he headed for the front door, he swung back in my direction, pointed the knife at me, and growled, "When I bring your family back here, that lasagna better be ready. And the cake too. That would make me feel a whole lot better, and you'd appreciate me feeling better, wouldn't you?" Then he stalked out of the room, and I heard the front door slam.

"He should have made sure no one could see him leave," muttered Beard to himself. Then he said to me, "You might as well cook the stuff he wants. It'll keep you out of my hair." He sat in a kitchen chair, took out his handkerchief, and started polishing the revolver.

Woodenly, I opened cupboards, taking out the ingredients for the cake and the lasagna. I felt despair wash over me. What on earth had prompted George to mention Florrisant? "There's a lot of territory around Florrisant," I softly repeated to myself, but it wasn't much comfort.

The phone rang. Once again I waited to find out who was calling. "Hi, Jane. It's Pam. Are you still there? We haven't done our visiting teaching yet this month. Do you want to try for tonight? Gotta run or I'll be late for church. I'll see you there. Bye."

# Chapter Four

"STOP WORKING FOR A FEW minutes, and sit right here so I can keep an eye on you," Beard said, waving the gun at the chair opposite him.

I sat obediently. The hours I'd spent in that chair had made me acutely aware of how uncomfortable it really was. The torn-up couch would have been preferable, but I wasn't about to give up the comparative freedom of the kitchen for the family room, where I'd been tied up. I decided that, when this was all over, I'd have to get some of those frilly cushions to tie on the chairs. My menfolk would just have to learn to like ruffles.

Once he was sure I was settled, Beard went into the family room and took a cell phone out of his jacket pocket. At first I was puzzled as to why he didn't just use my phone. Then the light dawned. Of course. He was worried about the fact that the phone company recorded all long-distance phone calls. We'd easily be able to trace his call to his boss when this was all over. He wasn't as dumb as the movies made gangsters out to be. But then, I'd never considered Beard to be stupid. Kid, now, was another story.

Beard turned away as he punched the buttons on his phone, but I realized he'd still be able to see me out of the corner of his eye. I tried to see which numbers he punched, but he had the phone tilted away from me. He said something into the phone, then listened, talked, listened. He seemed totally absorbed in his conversation. I wondered if he'd really notice if I moved. The door to the garage was right behind me—about six feet behind me. Could I make it to the door before he caught me? If I did, then what? Could I get out of the garage before he got out there too? The main door was operated by a garage door opener. If I hit the button as I went into the garage, I could probably scuttle under the door and run to Manny and Angela's house. Except Manny and Angela wouldn't be there. I looked at my watch. It was 11:12. Right then, they would be listening to a member of the bishopric make announcements in sacrament meeting. There would be no one to run to—at least, no one I could trust. As I mentioned before, the other neighbors weren't too friendly. Besides, Beard could probably run faster than I could over a long distance.

What if I were able to get out to the garage and into my van? That would be harder. My keys were in my purse close to the family room, so getting them was out of the question, but we always kept another set hanging on a hook above Art's workbench in the garage. If I got out into the garage, could I hit the garage door opener button, grab the keys, start the van, and back out before Beard could get to me? What if he shot at me? What if he tried to follow me? I assumed Kid had taken their only vehicle. If I could get into the van and away from the house, Beard wouldn't be able to follow me, and I could get to the police and have them waiting at the house when Kid got back. My heart beat faster at the thought of getting away. Could I do it? The way my heart was racing, I'd probably faint first.

*NOTE: Professor Mallory, I know you're wondering why I'm dragging this part out with all this thinking and no action. I'm trying to establish the fact that I'm not stupid and I really was looking for ways to escape all the time. Besides, the thinking part only really took about ten seconds, but if you don't like it, I can take it out.*

Beard was still talking on his phone. He glanced at me and then away to fumble in his shirt pocket for a pen and a 3 x 5 card. I inched my chair back from the table. Beard put the 3 x 5 card on the back of the couch to write on it. I stood slowly. Beard didn't seem to notice. He stuffed the pen and card back in his shirt pocket. His back was nearly turned toward me. I whirled on the ball of one foot to run out to the garage. He was still talking, although his voice sounded like he was finishing his conversation. I thought I'd better hurry.

I'd only taken two steps before I was startled to feel an all-too-familiar iron grip on my shoulder. I nearly screamed again, and Beard rasped in my ear, "Where do you think you're going?"

"The cake," I said, pointing to the oven, which was nearly in the direction I'd been going. "I was afraid it was burning." Indeed, the smell of well-done lemon cake was quite strong.

His fingers slowly relaxed. He nodded toward the oven. "OK. Look."

I bent over the open oven door for just a moment longer than I probably needed to because I was shaking so hard

I could hardly stand. I was so very disappointed that he'd caught me. If only I hadn't waited to run. If only I had been by the oven in the first place, I would have been closer to the garage door. If only . . . If only . . .

Beard was watching me, so I grabbed a couple of pot holders and brought the cake pans out. He settled himself at the table. After watching me turn the cake layers out onto the cooling racks, he went back into the family room to get some more financial files. At the rate he was going through everything, he would know more about Art's business than Art did. I fussed along the counter, putting things away and getting out the makings of the frosting, until I was close enough to my purse that I could quickly reach into its side pocket and retrieve my car keys. I slipped them into my pants pocket. Maybe if I'd had them on me I wouldn't have hesitated and would have been driving away at this very moment. I sighed, even though I knew it didn't do any good to beat myself up. Two clichés came to mind: "Don't cry over spilt milk" and "He who hesitates is lost." They were only too true.

I'm only an average to poor housekeeper by my mother's standards. Doing the same things over and over again bores me to tears. There are so many more interesting things to do than clean. Oh, every once in a while I go into a cleaning frenzy, and I do manage to keep the majority of mess out of sight, but nothing like my mother. She assigns certain chores to certain days of the week, and nothing gets in the way of getting those chores done. I don't know what's wrong with me, but I get easily distracted from housework by such little things as playing with the kids or reading a good book.

The only reason I'm telling you about my lack of housekeeping skills is that I'd decided the best way to get those two men off guard was to play the part of the perfect housekeeper—docile and proper, my mother to a T. Only, my mother had a hidden streak of feistiness in her—me too, actually, but I didn't want them to know that. To foster the perfect housekeeper image, I was constantly wiping down counters and walls, sweeping the floor, putting away dishes, and scrubbing the sink. My kitchen had never looked so good, and cleaning kept me up and moving around. I thought that if they were used to having me move around, it would give me more freedom and make getting away easier. It was also making me tired, as was my lack of sleep.

When I have visitors, I'm a good hostess for three days. I can keep the house clean and cook wonderful breakfasts, lunches, and dinners—for three days. Then I collapse, and my guests have to fend for themselves. I'd only been cooking and cleaning at full speed for less than twenty-four hours, and I was already exhausted. Food helped. I must admit I'd eaten my fair share of the cookies and everything else I'd cooked last night. My pants were getting tight around the waistband too, which meant my plan to climb out that small bathroom window was growing less and less plausible. Oh well. Something would happen, I was sure. I'd been praying and praying for help ever since I was first grabbed, and I had a feeling things were going to work out. I just didn't know how or when. I hoped that my idea of how and when was the same as the Lord's. Oftentimes it isn't, and I'm left wondering just how close to the fire I have to get. I've been burned pretty badly at times, but they say scar tissue is tougher than regular skin.

As I thought, my hands busied themselves with the ingredients for lasagna. I decided to make a lot, since we might be reduced to eating leftovers if these guys stayed here much longer. I had a great recipe I'd gotten from our ward Relief Society cookbook last year.

*NOTE: Professor Mallory, if you want the recipe I'd be happy to give it to you. Our Relief Society made a really neat cookbook, and the recipe's in there. I have several copies of the book left.*

If these guys didn't eat it all, there should be enough left for Kyle and his family when they came. I just hoped the food would hold out until I got rid of my captors. I was already trying to remember what I had in my food storage that would be good enough to soothe these two savage beasts. My mother had bottled some wonderful chili, which she'd given me because she knows I don't can unless I have someone to do it with. Mom lives in Blackfoot, Idaho, so I don't can or bottle or whatever. I always wondered why people called it canning when they used bottles. The tomato sauce I was using for the lasagna *was* in a can though, a commercial can. Actually, I was using tomato juice. I find that with a few spices thrown in, it makes great lasagna sauce because it cooks down, even though it starts out runny.

As I was thinking about the sauce, I was opening the can of tomato juice with the electric can opener. I hate opening large cans with the electric can opener because I have to hold the can over the edge of the counter while I do it, and I'm always afraid the can will slip. It didn't slip, but when the opener got around to where it had started, the lid flipped up and splattered red tomato juice all over my yellow scout shirt. I just stood there looking at it drip down my front. Disgusting.

Unexpectedly, I felt like crying. It's surprising how, when things are going badly, just one small unfortunate incident can make me lose it, even when I've been brave throughout the whole ordeal. A tear rolled down my cheek. I told myself to stop it. I didn't want Beard to see me cry. Another tear rolled down. I turned my back on Beard and tried staring at the ceiling. That sometimes helps in fast and testimony meeting when I get teary.

*NOTE: Professor Mallory, I'll have to explain about fast and testimony meeting in person. Just understand it can be a very tender experience.*

Another tear followed the first two. I stared harder. Then I noticed the spot on the ceiling where Brant had planted his foot while doing a handstand on the counter. And we had just finished painting the ceiling too. Kids. Sometimes I thought mine had brains the size of peas. I remembered when—

"Hey, you!" said Beard.

I turned around with dry eyes. I guess Brant's escapades were good for something.

"Come over here, and sit down." He motioned toward the chair I'd sat in all night.

I sighed and sat, eyes down, watching tomato juice dry on my shirt.

Beard thrust a bunch of papers under my nose. "Tell me about these."

The papers were just receipts for purchases Art had made for his store. What could Beard want with them? I looked up at Beard, bewildered by his request.

"Just tell me about them," he demanded.

"Well, the first is for some paint," I said.

He rolled his eyes. "I can see that. Tell me what it's for."

"It's for Art's store office. He got it from a professional supply warehouse because they gave him a great deal," I explained. Was that what he wanted to hear?

"One office wouldn't need that much paint. Why did he get so much?"

"Because he got a better price when he bought more. We used the rest on the house, like here in the kitchen, because it's a really tough grade of enamel," I said. Just not tough enough to withstand Brant's shoe, I thought.

He took that receipt and then pointed at the next one. "What's that?"

"Light fixtures for Art's store office, and we got five because we got a good deal. We used two of them in the family room."

"Hm." Beard grunted. He took that receipt and waited for me to explain the next one.

I continued, "Filing cabinets. Used army surplus. Very good deal, so we bought four. One of them is here in the family room, where you got these receipts."

He grunted again, took the filing-cabinet receipt, added it to his pile, and pointed at mine.

"The next one is for desk chairs. Same thing. The next one is for carpet. Good deal, so we bought enough for his office and the family room. The next one—"

"That's enough." Beard took the rest of the receipts from me. I waited, watching while he thumbed through them thoughtfully. After a few minutes, he handed back a couple. "What about those?"

I had to study them for a minute before I could answer. I could hardly make out what they said. Art's handwriting wasn't the best. It looked like something about used auto parts, quite a few too. The receipts were copies of handwritten ones, written out for one person but then written on again. It looked like "stolen" and "serial numbers," but it was only because I knew Art's handwriting so well that I could make out that part. Was that why Beard and Kid were after Art? Because of some used parts taken from stolen cars? Had Art

threatened to go to the police like he had when some teenage
gang members had tried to sell him stolen parts? I hoped
he hadn't been so stupid again. He should have just gone to
the police in the first place rather than trying to scare those
kids. Manny had told him it could have gotten dangerous.
Maybe now the dangerous part was happening. Handing
back the receipts, I shrugged. "They look like they're for used
car parts."

"What does that say?" Beard pointed to the newer writing
that I thought said "stolen."

"I'm not sure. Maybe serial numbers." I didn't dare say
anything about the parts being stolen.

Beard stared at the receipts as if trying to decipher Art's
handwriting himself. I wasn't worried that he would be able
to. Not even Jerry, Art's manager, can read my husband's
writing. Finally, Beard leaned forward, showing me one of
the receipts again. "Are you sure these are all car parts? What's
that one that starts with a C?"

I squinted at it. It certainly looked like a C, but the rest
of the word was a mystery to me. Shrugging, I said, "Maybe
clutch?"

The telephone rang. Beard watched me warningly while
it rang three more times. As soon as Art's message was over,
Pam's voice said, "Jane? Where are you? Are you OK? When
I saw that you weren't in Relief Society, I ducked out to
could call you. You haven't missed a meeting in years, so I'm
worried. If you don't call me soon, I'll go see our sisters by
myself, OK? Sure hope you're all right. Good-bye."

"She's pretty persistent. Is she your sister?" asked Beard.

"Yeah," I answered absently, glancing at the clock on the
wall. Relief Society would be about half over. Then everyone
would be out of church. Give them half an hour to get home,

and Manny and Pam and the rest would start calling again. I just hoped Beard wouldn't get too annoyed. I also hoped Kid was having a terrible time trying to find Art and the boys. I hoped it with all my heart. Kid had been gone nearly three hours, and it was all I could do to not bite my fingernails because of my anxiety.

The rain was still pouring down outside. It was a little late in the season for much snow, but it had been colder than usual this year. I hoped it was snowing hard wherever Art was because it would make it hard for Kid to find them and it would keep them inside their snow fort or igloo. They loved camping in the snow, and they'd gone prepared with dry firewood, down sleeping bags, and lots of goodies that didn't need cooking.

Camping is fine with me, but not in the snow. Too cold. Give me a nice hot summer day anytime. My husband and boys, though, were hot in any weather over sixty-five degrees and were constantly freezing me by opening the windows in the dead of winter. That reminded me of the snow again and Kid wandering around in the mountains looking for my family. Fear rose up in my throat like bile. I had to physically gulp it down and breathe deeply to calm myself. *Please*, I prayed, *please don't let anything happen to my family.*

Beard continued looking at the pile of receipts on the table in front of him, frowning at some, squinting at others. After several minutes I asked, "May I keep cooking?" On the off chance that Kid did find my family, I wanted all the food ready to sweeten him up and to give my menfolk something to eat besides. Beard nodded.

Moving around in the kitchen helped me calm down some. Having mundane tasks to busy my fingers was thera- peutic. I filled a pot with water for the lasagna noodles and set it on the stove, adding a little salt. It was a good thing I hadn't already started the noodles cooking or they'd have been mush by then. I added olive oil to the water and turned the burner to high. Then, while the water was heating, I started browning the hamburger. Next I tried scrubbing the tomato juice off my shirt, without much luck. It had left big red stains that weren't going to come out without the stain remover downstairs in my laundry room. I sighed. Oh well. It wasn't as if anyone was going to see me except Beard and Kid. That is, unless the police crashed through the front door. Then maybe they would think Beard or Kid had shot me or something. Now if only I could figure out a way to get the police and my captors together.

By the time I was layering noodles, meat, and cheese in my biggest lasagna pan, the phone had started ringing again: first Manny, then my visiting teachers—each at a different time—then Pam just before she went to see the sisters we visited. Each time the phone rang, I stopped what I was doing and turned to listen to the answering machine, only to find Beard staring at me. What was he thinking? What was he planning? I wished I knew.

The smell of lasagna was starting to fill the kitchen when Manny called again. At the sound of the voice, Beard turned to me, looking extremely annoyed. I shrugged. What could I do to stop Manny from calling? Resigned to another question about home teaching, I leaned against the counter to listen. This time Manny's message wasn't only about home teaching though.

"Sorry we missed didn't make it over there today, Jane. I guess we'll just have to count when you and your family came to dinner at the beginning of the month; although, getting it done that early just doesn't seem like real home teaching." He chuckled. I could almost see his eyes twinkling. For a police-man, he was surprisingly cheerful. He went on, "Angela and I were wondering if you'd like to join us at the Memorial Day picnic and concert. George told me Art and the boys went camping so you'll be alone, and we'd like you to come. Actually, you'd be going with Angela and the kids because I have to work. Anyway, let us know. We hope you can. The kids love you, and they behave better when you're around." He laughed and hung up.

Beard's face was dark red, and he looked extremely fed up. He started to say something, stopped, said, "You have the most irritating friends imaginable," and then snapped his jaw shut—only he didn't say it quite that politely.

I had to turn to slide the lasagna into the oven and busy myself with the cake frosting to keep my laughter from bubbling out. What was wrong with me? First I cried over tomato juice, and then I felt like laughing uncontrollably. Must be stress. I'd felt the same way when Art was in the hospital.

The nice thing about lasagna is that it isn't hurt by staying in the oven for a few hours, which was good because Kid didn't get back until nearly five. He was cold, wet, surly, and hungry, but most importantly, he was alone. When he walked through the door all by himself—no Art, no boys—I sagged against the kitchen counter and sent up a silent prayer of thanks.

Throwing his soaked leather jacket onto the couch, Kid announced belligerently, "Not a sign of them anywhere. It's a blizzard up there. There must be at least a foot of new snow." He plopped into a kitchen chair, eyeing Beard warily.

I did too. I guess we both expected the older man to explode. Instead, he only said, "Never mind. The snow will drive them down out of the mountains, and we'll be waiting for them."

Wave after wave of relief washed over me so intensely I had to go over to the sink and fuss with some dishes. In my mind's eye, I was picturing Art and the boys snug in their igloo with a fire burning brightly, the dog snuggled up to Art, its favorite person in the world. It was a comforting picture.

Kid grabbed a handful of the M&M cookies I'd made. I'd had to take the lasagna out for ten minutes at a time for each sheet of cookies, but it hadn't hurt the lasagna any. He took a bite of cookie then opened the oven door and sniffed appreciatively. "When's dinner?"

"It's ready now," I answered.

"Good. I've been looking forward to this all day," he said, seating himself at the table and laying his knife next to his plate just as if it were part of the silverware. I couldn't help standing there staring at him. He looked good sitting there all by himself, even with his knife. No Art. No boys. Very good.

# Chapter Five

"DORINDA!" EXCLAIMED SPENCER TRACY (JOE) as he hurriedly got up from the table to greet Irene Dunne (Dorinda).

"Dorinda!" mocked Kid, bursting into his machine-gun laughter. He'd found my stash of DVDs and was seated comfortably in the recliner watching *A Guy Named Joe* and eating more of my Häagen-Dazs. "Have you ever heard such a dorky name in your life? Dorky Dorinda. Heh! Heh! Heh! Heh! Heh!"

I wanted to clobber him. I'm afraid my kinder tendencies had been destroyed. I'm sure Beard would have wanted to as well, but he was in the shower. Kid was supposed to be making sure I didn't escape, so I had to sit on the torn-up couch, where he could watch me as well as the television. He was eating the caramel praline ice cream, one of my favorites. Of course, most of the Häagen-Dazs's flavors are my favorites.

Sitting on the couch wouldn't have been too bad except I had to be near Kid and his knife, which he threatened me with every once in a while. I was tired of standing or sitting at the table in the kitchen. After that hard kitchen chair, even a torn-up couch felt wonderful—a little too wonderful. I wanted to fall asleep; not even being threatened with the knife could keep me awake. I'd probably only gotten four or five hours of sleep the night before. My head nodded, and my eyelids closed for a few minutes, only to be jerked open again when Kid exploded, "Girl clothes! Give me a break!"

I glanced at the television. Irene Dunne had just opened the box Spencer Tracy had given her and was holding up the clothes he'd bought for her. I couldn't see why Kid thought they were so strange. They looked pretty good to me. I identified completely with Irene Dunne's reaction to the clothes, especially since I'd been wearing a dirty Cub Scout den leader uniform for over twenty-four hours. Was it only twenty-four hours? It felt like a lifetime.

Staring sightlessly at the television, I wondered at my situation. No one I knew would ever believe I was sitting there at the mercy of two thugs, who obviously had some evil agenda concerning my family, specifically my husband. I could hardly believe it myself. What could they possibly want? I kept going back to the idea of the stolen car parts. After all, Beard had set those receipts aside rather too casually. That could have been so I wouldn't attach any importance to them. If that was the case, I thought, I'd better start remembering everything Art had told me when he'd figured out the car parts were stolen.

The first time was nearly three years ago, while Evan was on his mission and Brant was giving us nightmares over his behavior. It was clear in my mind because having stolen parts unloaded on us was just one more thing we had to deal with during a several-month period I can only describe as purgatory.

I think I realized it was turning into a dark era in our lives when a neighbor called to tell me she'd noticed Brant at the mall with some other boys during school hours. I'd hoped it was just something most fourteen-year-olds had to do once in their lives, but deep inside, I knew it meant real trouble. There were other signs that disaster was about to strike. Brant had started complaining about going to church, getting his hair cut, and doing his chores. I'd gotten calls from his teachers about missing assignments. Of course, my other boys had all done similar things at one point or another, but with them it was more of a game to see how much they could get away with. Not Brant. He was moody, and his complaints had a fierceness to them that spoke of deeper troubles. Neither Art nor I wanted to acknowledge our fears openly though. At that point in our lives, things were really looking good after years of struggle. Art's shop was finally prospering so well he'd had to bring in a manager and hire two more mechanics.

Our family life was nearly perfect as well. Kyle had been married for two years, and he and Veronica had a darling little girl—who Art and I were absolutely batty about—and another on the way. Evan was over halfway through with his mission in Ecuador and doing wonderfully. Jimmy, our youngest son, was an absolutely delightful eleven-year-old involved in every possible sport and doing well in school besides. Art was in the bishopric, and I was Young Women president. We were all busy and happier than anyone had a right to be. The only fly in the ointment was Brant.

To tell you the truth, I was almost grateful for Brant's small rebellions. Things were *too* good, and it was making me nervous. I have a theory about good times that's never failed yet. It's that if you aren't in the middle of some test or other, you're just getting ready for a real doozer—and what a doozer, or combination of doozers, the next few tests turned out to be.

Art and I had a gentle talk with Brant about families and responsibilities and the importance of the gospel. But I don't think it even got past his eardrums, although things went a little more smoothly for a while. Then one day he simply didn't come home. After calling frantically and searching the neighborhood, we had only one clue as to his whereabouts: someone had heard he was staying with a friend in another part of town, but they didn't know who. We didn't know he even knew anyone in a different part of town. We didn't have time to find out either.

The next day we got a call from Evan's mission president saying Evan would be coming home early because he'd become deathly ill. *Deathly ill* is not a term to calm a mother's heart, but it was exactly what Evan looked like when he stumbled off the plane two days later, helped by a couple of returning missionaries on either side of him who were terribly relieved to turn him over to us. At first the doctors thought he'd contracted parasites, even though he swore he'd been careful about his drinking water and washing his vegetables and such. Further tests revealed a nasty infection—one resistant to antibiotics. They only let us take him home from the hospital because I convinced them I was good at nursing my sons back to health and because I promised to follow their directions implicitly.

In the middle of all this, Jimmy broke his leg in a ball game, and we ended up back in the hospital in the emergency room. Because Art's business was so busy and since he was in the bishopric, most of the responsibility for sickroom care fell on me. So there I was, waiting hand and foot on Evan, who could hardly keep anything down, and Jimmy, who couldn't sleep and couldn't get around because of his broken leg. Whenever I wasn't fussing over Evan or Jimmy, I was thinking about Brant.

If it hadn't been for our friends from church, I don't know what kind of basket case I would have been. My visiting teachers arranged to have lovely dinners brought in two or three nights a week.

*NOTE: Professor Mallory, that is one of the things visiting teachers do. I'll explain more later, if you want.*

Sister Mellancamp, a sweet older woman, brought fresh flowers from her garden every few days. Evan really enjoyed them. Manny mowed our lawn and said he'd keep an eye out for Brant. My counselors in Young Women simply took over so I wouldn't have to worry about activities or lessons.

*NOTE: I'll explain about Young Women too, if you'd like. Whew! I had no idea everything in my life revolved around the Church so much.*

Even with all that help, the strain was still pretty heavy—which was why it seemed like the last straw when Art bought some parts from what he thought was a reputable wrecking yard, only to realize they were stolen. When he checked with the wrecking yard, they said they'd never heard of the guys who'd sold the parts. Art was disgusted when he came home that night—disgusted with himself for being so gullible and with the guys who'd sold him the parts for being dishonest. He said he should have realized they were too young to be representing an established business. I tried to console him by pointing out that a lot of younger guys liked to mess around with cars, so it wasn't unusual to be dealing with young men in their late teens or early twenties, but Art wanted none of it. He was going to be gloomy no matter what.

There was too much bad stuff happening—Evan wasn't doing much better in spite of all the medicine he was taking, Jimmy had weeks until he would be any better, and we still hadn't heard from Brant. To make matters worse, Kyle called that very night from Texas to say that the wonderful company that had hired him straight out of college and moved him to Texas had just laid him off. Art and I both went to bed discouraged.

Things gradually improved after that. The next day, Art turned the stolen parts over to the police, and the antibiotic finally seemed to make some headway against Evan's infection. Within another week, Jimmy had figured out how to do tricks on his crutches that had us gasping with laughter and fear for his safety. I think he mainly did his stunts to make Evan smile. It certainly seemed to cheer him up.

Kyle found an even better job close to his new home, and every once in a while, one of the boys in our ward would call to say they'd seen Brant; although, he avoided them so they never got to talk to him. At least we knew he was alive and still in the area. Art drove around to where the boys had said they'd seen Brant, but he never did see our son. That alone was enough to depress us. There were many mornings when I woke up with red, puffy eyes and Art went off to work with a grim look on his face. Then things started to improve a little more.

I had a real shock one day when I came home from a quick run to the store to find Brant seated on Evan's bed talking to him. I was about to rush in to grab him and either shake him or hug him when I caught Evan's eye. He gave me a look that said, "Don't blow this by overreacting or you'll never see him again."

Forewarned, I said, "Hello, Brant. Do you want some ice cream? I was just going to get some for Evan."

Brant shrugged. "Sure, whatever," he said and turned to resume his conversation with Evan. That was it. That was all he said to his loving mother after giving me days and nights filled with anxiety. I could have killed him, but I was afraid I'd never find out where he'd been.

That wasn't the last time Brant went off like that, and it always seemed to be at the worst times, but at least I knew he would probably be all right. One time I talked to one of the parents of a boy Brant stayed with from time to time. I thanked the man for taking care of my son, even though the words stuck in my throat. The man replied, "Brant is always welcome. He's such a good influence on our boy—so polite and helpful around the house." I nearly choked. If Brant was a good example, with his shaved head, chains, knives, earrings, and black leather, I hated to think what that man's son was like.

Then months later, just when we were seeing daylight again, an even greater disaster struck—struck in every sense of the word. Art was putting a new engine into a car when the chain holding it to the winch broke, and the engine swung down, crushing Art's chest. If it hadn't been for one of the mechanics administering mouth-to-mouth and a blessing, I'm sure Art would have died right there. I'll forever be grateful that Evan wrote home months before and asked if Art would hire the young man, who'd been one of Evan's favorite companions, so he could earn money to go to college. We thought he was pretty sharp when we first met him, but his quick thinking that day was really impressive.

*NOTE: As I said earlier, Professor Mallory, if you have any questions about any of this, just ask.*

I already wrote about the days and nights in the hospital watching over Art, so I won't go into that again. In the long months it took for Art to heal, we completely forgot about the stolen auto parts. It wasn't until several months after he'd returned to work that anyone tried to sell him stolen parts again. Jerry, his manager, said that no one had tried while Art was in the hospital either. But in the two to three months previous to when Beard and Kid showed up, there had been at least two times. The first time Art had paid them and then immediately turned the parts over to the police, being very careful to preserve the fingerprints. The second time, however, the guys selling the parts had been young, and Art thought he'd give them a second chance. So he'd told them not to come back or he'd call the police. Like I said, I wished he'd have just turned everything over to the police in the first place. If he had, I wouldn't have been sitting there on that couch with Kid watching me and *A Guy Named Joe* at the same time.

"What are you doing?" Kid thrust his knife up against my throat.

I jumped and stared at Kid with startled eyes. He was looking down at my hands. I looked too. Of their own accord, my hands were plucking at the stuffing coming out of the couch cushion. I pulled the errant fingers back on my lap, not knowing what to say—fearing to say the wrong thing. The last thing I wanted was for that knife to get any closer to my throat.

"Heh! Heh! Heh! Heh! Scared you, didn't I?" Kid laughed, pulling his knife back to lie in his lap.

I nodded. Where was Beard? At least with him around, Kid wasn't outright malicious. That's all I needed on top of everything else—to have Kid begin tormenting me in earnest. Somehow I knew he was capable of terrible cruelty, and it made me very nervous.

"Would you like some homemade fudge sauce to go on top of the ice cream?" I asked, hoping to divert his attention.

He looked interested.

"I make it myself with real chocolate from a recipe my mother gave me. She's won prizes for her fudge sauce." That was an outright lie. My mother wouldn't touch chocolate with a ten-foot pole. She's a health nut who eats nothing but all-natural, no-sugar, no-fat foods. I think the reason I'm so hefty and such a good cook is in reaction to a childhood where the sweetest thing to eat was the fruit leather my mother made—without sugar, of course. Angela and I had concocted the recipe for this fudge sauce for a Relief Society All-Chocolate Night, and it had won rave reviews. We called it Pure-Sin Chocolate Fudge Sauce. The name was a hit too.

"Yeah, why don't you fill up the empty part of the carton with that fudge sauce." He thrust the carton of Häagen-Dazs into my hand as I stood. I could hear my joints creaking as they unfolded, and I felt pain shoot through my legs. I couldn't remember the last time I was so sore over every inch of my body, especially my back and legs and feet. Sleeping at the table and standing to cook all day had done a job on me, that's for sure.

As I was plodding into the kitchen, Kid yelled in a voice dripping with sarcasm, "And hurry it up, old lady. I put the movie on pause while you're getting my fudge sauce, and I just can't wait to see what happens next. Something tells me that that Dorinda babe is going to do something really dumb.

Dumb, dorky Dorinda." He finished with his machine-gun laugh.

"Forget the fudge sauce," said Beard from the bathroom door, looking clean and refreshed. "We're going to take a little ride down to the auto parts store, all three of us."

# Chapter Six

THIS TIME IT REALLY WAS a dark and stormy night, although I could tell by the way the clouds were scudding in front of the moon that it would be clear by tomorrow. The storm outside would be past, but not my storm. That took longer to clear up. We stepped out into the backyard into a tremendous spring wind storm like only Colorado Springs can have. Colorado Springs is the only place I've ever lived where they actually name the weather, and I can see why they do. Winds that are commonly over sixty miles an hour deserve to be named. Even with my jacket on, I gasped as the wind hit me full in the face. I was glad Beard had insisted I wear the jacket to cover up my bright yellow Cub Scout shirt. At least it offered some protection. I could tell from the way Kid hunched over that he was regretting how wet his leather jacket still was. Beard had an L.L.Bean navy blue jacket with huge pockets. I'd seen him slip the gun into one. He was probably the warmest one in our trio.

Kid took the lead, presumably because he knew where he'd left their car. I followed, with Beard's hand gripping my shoulder as he brought up the rear. When we reached the gate to the backyard, Kid slipped out while Beard held me back. Kid came back long enough to say the coast was clear before he left again, and we followed. Not for the first time, I cursed the stingy city council for refusing to put streetlights on our street. It was dark except when the moon peeked out from behind the flying clouds every other minute or so. We kept to lawns and beside hedges or trees as we made our way down the street, I guess so we wouldn't be silhouetted against the light pavement of the sidewalks. Unfortunately, we went in the opposite direction from where Manny and Angela lived, although I don't know what good it would have done me to go near their house. For all I knew they were still out doing their home and visiting teaching.

The car was parked on the next street over. Kid got in the driver's seat. Beard pushed me into the backseat and followed me in. Then he gave Kid directions on how to get to the auto parts store. It was frightening to realize how well Beard knew the way to the store. If he knew it that well, why didn't he just go by himself? Maybe Beard didn't trust Kid on his own with me at my house (for which I was grateful) or on his own at the auto parts store. But what could Beard possibly want at the auto parts store? All I could think of was that Art hadn't brought the business receipts home since last month, and perhaps Beard had noticed they weren't in the files. Maybe Beard wanted to look through more files and thought they'd be at the store.

Traffic was light, even for a Sunday night. All the businesses near the auto parts store were dark, so no one was there to see us drive around to the back. Beard had found

Art's spare set of keys in his desk at home, so now he opened the door to the garage and ushered us inside. I was hoping he'd be stupid enough to turn the lights on, but he wasn't. Instead, he took a small flashlight from his jacket pocket, shined it around only enough to find the door to the store, and then turned it off. We groped toward the door in the dark. I heard the sound of another key in a lock and a door opening; then I was shoved toward the sound. Kid had taken over ushering me around, and he wasn't too gentle about it. My foot hit what felt like the rail for the car lift in the bay closest to the store. It hurt like blazes, but I didn't say anything. I just gritted my teeth and limped as little as I could. I didn't want to appear any more vulnerable than I already did. It might give them ideas.

Once we were all inside the store, Beard turned on the little flashlight just long enough to locate the office. In the residual glow from the tiny beam, the familiar store seemed alien, almost repulsive. I shivered as I was shoved once more from behind. Beard switched off the flashlight and entered the office, with Kid pushing me once more. I could hear Beard moving around in the room. He turned his little flashlight on briefly, picked up the lid from a box of paper by the copier, and taped the cardboard over the window in the office door with some regular office tape. Then he switched on the overhead light and finished sealing the lid to the door with some duct tape that had been on the desk. When he stepped back to survey his handiwork, he shook his head, grabbed a couple of pillows from the couch, and laid them across the crack at the bottom of the door. Although the door was plainly visible through the front window from the street, no one would be able to tell the light was on.

"Sit," he said to me, indicating the couch. I sat.

The office was a mess, as it usually was whenever I hadn't been there for a while. I may not be the best housekeeper in the world, but whenever I worked in the office, I left it immaculate. It was obvious I hadn't been here for a long time. No wonder Art hadn't brought home the receipts for nearly two months. He probably couldn't find them. Art had never lost a receipt yet, although he'd come close. They were probably somewhere in the room. But it would take several hours of straightening and filing before the business's records were in order again. I sighed. Right then I didn't care. The only positive side was that as messy as this place was, Beard's chance of finding anything worthwhile was very slim.

Beard evidently thought so too. He pointed to the desk and told Kid, "You try to find every bill and receipt you can in that junk, and organize it by date while I go through the filing cabinet. Be sure to keep an eye out for anything else that might be valuable too." He gave Kid a you-know-what-I-mean look. I wondered what he meant.

"Why can't you do it while I go through the filing cabinet?" whined Kid. I hate whiners.

Beard just gave him a withering look. "Because you don't know what to look for. But you can read and count, or haven't you learned how yet?"

Kid just stared at him sullenly then started sifting through the papers on the desk. I watched as they worked, thinking that another bonus was that most of my filing work might be done for me if Kid really could read. They worked steadily for about forty minutes according to the office clock. Every once in a while, Beard pulled out a file folder and laid it in a growing pile. He periodically checked Kid's work but seemed satisfied for the most part. They both stood where they could easily watch me as they worked. I don't know what they thought I could do. Throw pillows at them?

At 11:34 p.m., Beard glanced at the clock and grunted. He picked up an Art's Parts plastic bag lying on the floor and stuffed the file folders and receipts into it. "OK, let's go," he said.

Restraining a groan, I heaved myself up off the couch. Even forty minutes of sitting hadn't helped lessen my soreness any. Beard turned out the light in the office then slowly opened the door, and we followed him through the darkness back out to the car.

The drive back to the house was as silent in the car as it was on the streets. We saw only one vehicle, and it turned on to a side street before we actually got to it. When we were about halfway home, the horrible thought occurred to me that perhaps my family had come home while we were gone. My stomach tightened again, so hard I felt nauseated. *Please don't let that be true*, I prayed. *Please keep my family safe.* I didn't care what happened to me as long as nothing happened to my family.

To my relief, the house was dark except for the faint glow of a lamp in the family room. Beard had decided to leave that light on all the time so people would think it was like a night light we left on while we were on vacation. Kid parked the car on a different street from where it had been before, so we had to trudge across more lawns and skirt more trees and bushes than we had when we'd left, but I didn't care. I was just glad to get into my own empty home.

For the first time, Beard acted like he was tired. He rubbed his hand across the back of his neck as he plopped the shopping bag onto the kitchen table. "Go into the bathroom and hurry up," he told me.

I wondered at his solicitude but was glad to comply. Even while hurrying, I managed to check out a couple of drawers in the bathroom to see if they still had some things in them that I remembered being there. With a bunch of boys in the family, it was possible to find all kinds of things in bathroom drawers. Satisfied with what I'd found, I left the room.

*NOTE: Professor Mallory, I don't want to tell what I found in the bathroom at this point because it would ruin the surprise. What do you think?*

I soon found out why Beard had been so solicitous. As soon as I went back into the family room, I saw he'd been into Art's closet and had gotten most of the ties out.

"Lie down on the floor," Beard said, pointing to a spot in front of the couch.

Involuntarily, I could feel my face tightening into stubborn lines. No way was I going to lie down on the floor.

"I mean it," he insisted, pulling the gun out of his jacket pocket and pointing it at me. "Get down there."

Slowly, I lowered myself to the floor. Jerking me into a prone position, Beard used Art's ties to tie my hands while Kid tied my feet. Once more I was feeling like a trussed pig. My heart pounded with fear. I hated feeling like I was helpless. I tried to calm myself by remembering that they had had ample opportunity to do anything they wanted, and so far, besides that slap, threatening me, and tying me up on the recliner, all they'd done is eat and go through files.

With the job of tying me up done to his satisfaction, Beard rubbed the back of his neck again then passed his hand over his eyes. He yawned. "I get the couch tonight. You got it last night," he told Kid. Beard flopped onto the couch, sat up, stuffed some of the stuffing back into one cushion, and lay back down. Kid glared at him for a minute then sat in the recliner and pushed it back until he was lying down as well. He pulled the afghan over him that my mother had made for my birthday, but he kept one arm out, his hand clutching the monstrous knife. I'd have to wash the afghan two or three times before I'd feel good about using it again. In a few minutes, both of them were breathing lightly and evenly. They were asleep.

I was left to stare at the ceiling. There was a spot directly above me that was patterned differently from the rest. It was where Brant had picked up Jimmy and stuck his hair into the fresh plaster when we'd textured the ceiling.

I was grateful the floor wasn't too hard. When we'd put in the new carpet, we'd gotten the super-deluxe padding. Brant and Jimmy loved to lie on it to watch television. They said it was like lying in bed, but at that moment, my bones and muscles and every other cell in my body were telling me that they were old—very old and very uncomfortable. I didn't know if I could endure an entire night of lying in one position. Besides, it was chilly, and I felt like I was coming down with a cold.

From where I was lying, I could see the time on the DVD player. It said it was 12:30. That meant it was 12:40. When we'd first gotten the player a few weeks ago, Jimmy had played with it and set the time ten minutes slow. Since then, we hadn't been able to figure out how to change it to the right time, so we just lived with it.

I glanced back up at the ceiling to the imprint of Jimmy's head. When we'd painted and put in the new carpet, we'd felt reasonably safe painting away evidences of the boys' younger childhood and Kyle and Evan's teenage years, including a hole where one of them had put his foot through the wall while they were wrestling. After all, two of the worst offenders were grown-up, and Jimmy was an adolescent. We should have waited at least a couple of years more. While lying on the floor, I couldn't help thinking that, up until that moment,

I had been looking forward to covering over the remaining boy-inflicted scars on our poor house as soon as Jimmy was a little older, like when he was gone on a mission, but while I was staring at his head print, I was overwhelmed with affection for that sign of his individuality and love of life. *Please*, I prayed, *keep Jimmy safe and Brant and Art and Evan and Kyle and . . .* I fell asleep praying.

The DVD player read 3:57 when I woke again. Someone was snoring. I think it was Beard because he shifted and the snoring stopped. Either the snoring or my aching body had wakened me. The snoring had been quiet, and I was used to Art snoring, so I decided it must have been the pain. I rolled onto my side, hoping for relief. It helped a little. What I really needed was to be untied and to take a shower and have a good night's sleep in my own bed. To do that, I would need to get away from Beard and Kid somehow—not just get away, get them caught by the police. I reviewed my plan in my head. It all revolved around getting them to trust me in some measure, to accept the things I'd been doing as normal and no cause for concern. It also revolved around Beard and Kid being very tired. It also revolved around the turkey I had in the basement freezer.

I thought it shouldn't be hard to convince Kid to get the turkey for me, though I shuddered about him going into other parts of my house. But if that's what it took, so be it. He'd have to get it early in the morning so I could get the turkey thawed in time to cook it for dinner. While I was refining my plans, fatigue took over, and I fell asleep again.

The next time I woke up, it was 5:18. I started to turn over and go back to sleep when I had a wonderful idea, an idea that would ensure that Beard and Kid didn't get enough sleep but wouldn't be angry with me for waking them up.

One of the television stations in our area comes on the air at 5:30 every morning. The best part was that to accommodate some of the US Army and Air Force personnel around Colorado Springs, the station starts out each day with a rousing rendition of the national anthem. I'd found out just how rousing one morning when I'd fallen asleep holding a much younger Jimmy, who'd been sick. We'd been watching a movie on that channel to get Jimmy's mind off his illness and had fallen asleep. When the national anthem came on in the morning, it had shocked us literally into standing at attention. I still remember how Jimmy and I had collapsed back onto the old couch in a heap, laughing until we got the hiccups. I was pretty sure the television station still followed the same procedure.

Eyeing the television speculatively, I decided that if I inched myself forward just a foot or two, I should be able to reach the power button with my toe. Thank goodness our new television had buttons and not dials like the old one. If I was quick, I could also press the volume button to lower the sound until I found the right station.

I humped forward like an inchworm, willing myself not to grunt. It wasn't easy to move someone my size quietly, especially with as much pain as I was feeling. With every little bit of progress, I stopped for a moment to make sure Beard and Kid hadn't woken up. My heart was up in my throat with each variation in their breathing. Who knows what they would think if they caught me so far from where they'd put me the night before.

When I was close enough, I raised my bound feet. By straining at Art's ties around my ankles, I could get the toe of one shoe on the power button and the toe of the other on the volume. Nearly overcome by the effort and suspense, I gritted my teeth and squinched my eyes nearly shut as I pressed with both toes. The television came on instantly, but before it was warmed up enough to make any sound, the green sound indicator at the bottom of the screen was already moving down to the lowest part of its range. I sagged in relief. Then I moved my toe over to the channel buttons and chose the right channel. Sure enough, it was showing a countdown clock with less than thirty seconds to go. Surprised, I realized I'd forgotten about the DVD player being ten minutes slow. I hurriedly pushed the volume up to full blast and then scrambled back to the couch and to the position I'd been in when Beard and Kid had fallen asleep.

Shivering with nervousness, I lay there with my eyes shut, counting down the seconds. Five, four, three, two, one. Nothing. Nothing. I peeked out of one eye. I was off by four seconds. I quickly shut my eyes again. "TA-DA-DA-DA-DA-DA-A-A," blared the television louder than I'd ever heard it go before.

"What the . . . ?!" yelled Beard and Kid at the same time.

*NOTE: That's not really what they said, and neither is the next little bit of conversation, but I already explained about my literary standards.*

They both leaped to their feet. One of them stepped on my leg.

"Ouch!" I yelped.

"What'd you leave that on for?" Beard yelled at Kid as he turned off the television by punching the power button with his fist, using the hand with the broken pinky finger. I winced. That couldn't have felt very good. It also couldn't have been very good for the television set. I hoped it wasn't broken—the set, not his fist.

"Me! You're always blaming me for everything!" Kid yelled back. He looked like he'd like to hit Beard. He waved his knife around menacingly.

"It's usually your fault!" Beard looked like he'd like to hit Kid, but the knife was making him cautious. This was even better than I'd hoped, except if they fought, they'd probably step on me some more. Even if they did, I didn't dare say anything or I'd call attention to myself. My muscles tensed in case I had to move out of their way quickly; then I decided I couldn't do that or they'd know how well I could move even though I was tied up. I had a hard time trying not to laugh hysterically. I kept seeing them leaping up from the couch and the recliner with terror-stricken faces, and now they were both waving their hands with identically broken fingers and yelling at each other. It was almost more than I could bear. I had to stare at Jimmy's head print on the ceiling and bite my lower lip. That calmed me some.

"Just forget it. I don't want any more of your excuses," Beard was saying with a clenched jaw. He turned on his heel, nearly tripped over me, and stalked into the kitchen. Then he stalked back with one of my sharpest kitchen knives and slashed through Art's ties, freeing my wrists and ankles. For the first time, I noticed that one of them was the fish tie Evan had given Art for Christmas. He'd gotten it at BYU, where he was a student. I'd have to call him and have him buy another one. It was one of Art's favorites.

"Get up!" growled Beard, and when I didn't move fast enough, he jerked me to my feet. He was in a very bad mood. I thought a small groan would be good for the helpless image as I rubbed feeling back into my arms, so I groaned. Hopefully, it helped the two men feel I couldn't possibly have gotten to the television set while in such a pitiful state. Besides, I felt like groaning as I tried to move. I felt like groaning a lot. He gave me a shove toward the kitchen. "Since we're up, you might as well make us some breakfast."

"Yeah!" Kid agreed, pointing the knife at me. "And make it a big one. I'm starved."

I hurried into the kitchen as fast as my poor body could make it so I wouldn't burst out laughing or crying. I couldn't decide which. After all Kid had eaten the day before, he was starved. Now the problem was finding something for them to eat. All the bacon was gone from the meat compartment in the refrigerator, but that was actually for the best. Turning to Kid, who had followed me into the kitchen, I said, "The only bacon that's left is in the freezer downstairs. Can I go get it?"

Kid looked at Beard for approval, and the older man nodded. I headed for the stairs with Kid right behind me, his knife held at the ready. My back felt nervous knowing that the point of that knife was only inches away. When we got to the freezer, I opened up the door, took out the bacon, and then paused.

"What's the matter?" asked Kid suspiciously, his knife inching closer to me.

"Nothing. I was just thinking you might like a turkey dinner tonight."

His face brightened. I almost felt guilty. This was too easy. He said, "Yeah? With pie and stuffing and cranberry sauce and everything?"

I nodded. "Even homemade crescent rolls and mashed potatoes and gravy." The rolls and potatoes were almost as important as the turkey.

He started to grin. "Is that the turkey in there?"

I nodded again. "But if we want it for tonight, I'll have to start thawing it out now."

"OK." Kid pulled out the turkey and carried it up the stairs behind me. I was impressed by how easily he carried it.

That bird weighed over twenty pounds, but then, he'd carried me just as easily. "Guess what," he announced to Beard. "We're having turkey dinner tonight."

Beard just shook his head. "Don't you ever fill up?"

"Not with food like this around." Kid patted the frozen turkey almost lovingly.

I showed him where I wanted it in the sink so I could run water over it. I used warm water, which isn't the safest way, but it's quicker than the cold-water method. Besides, I didn't much care if they did get botulism or whatever it is you can get from poultry. Then I busied myself cooking pancakes. It was a good thing I'd gotten so many eggs. I'd already used nearly three dozen. I had a couple of dozen more, which I figured ought to get me through the rest of the day, and after that, if my plan worked like I thought it would, it wouldn't matter. I could just go to the store and get more. And I'd need to with Kyle and Veronica and the girls coming.

After breakfast I started making pies. I was amazed at how much energy I had. I can only attribute that to help from above because I hadn't even gotten as much sleep as Beard and Kid. There's also a good possibility that I was energized by the thought of actually carrying out my plan. I'd planned and fretted so hard for a day and a half that it was heady stuff to sense that something positive might be about to happen. I'd often heard that "the Lord helps those who help themselves" and that a person is supposed to "pray as if everything depended upon the Lord, and work as if everything depended on you," which is why I tried so hard to work out a plan.

Somehow, though, those tried-and-true homilies didn't quite sit right. Somewhere in the back of my mind I kept remembering all the times in the scriptures when the Lord says He'll save the Israelites or do other things in his own due time. What if I wasn't supposed to get out of this mess for a long time? What if it was another lesson for me? I tried to push that thought to the back of my mind. I preferred to think of carrying out some plan of action rather than sitting around patiently and waiting until the Lord saw fit to rescue me. Maybe the Lord was inspiring me to think of a plan. There was that to think of as well. Oh, I was confused as confused could be. It was a good thing I had pies to bake to keep my hands busy or I would have gone crazy.

One apple pie and two pumpkin pies later, I was just sliding the turkey into the oven when Beard's cell phone started chirping. He heaved himself up out of the recliner and grabbed it out of his jacket pocket.

Kid smirked at his partner while licking his fingers clean of cinnamon and sugar from the leftover dough cookies he'd been eating. He indicated Beard with a movement of his knife. "Must be the boss. He's the only one who knows the number. Made him jump quick enough. Heh. Heh. Heh. Heh. Heh."

Beard turned just far enough away so we couldn't read his lips, just as he had the last time he'd spoken on the phone. He seemed to be in a serious conversation with the boss. At one point he raised his free hand to wipe his forehead. Could he be sweating? Must be serious indeed. I glanced over at Kid, who seemed to have forgotten all about dough cookies and was watching Beard intently. Kid's eyes narrowed as he watched. His whole countenance changed. His body stiffened. It was like watching the transformation from Dr. Jekyll into Mr. Hyde. Kid had been just a big, naughty boy a few minutes ago, playing tough guy, licking up sugar and cinnamon. Now he was more than naughty. He was bad. He was evil. I shivered. How could cooking a turkey dinner compete with something like that?

Beard, too, had changed. He crisply shoved the phone into his jacket pocket. His shoulders were set; his face was harder than I'd ever seen it. Who was this boss that he could have such an effect on two men? I began to be afraid of him—him specifically, not just some ethereal somebody out there. I didn't know his name, but he was suddenly very real. Somebody who could jerk people around according to his merest whim.

"All right. Let's go. Get your coat, Kid, and anything else you might have brought in with you. We're clearing out," barked Beard, shoving his arms into his jacket's sleeves.

My heart thudded to a stop. Clearing out?

"What?" Kid rose out of his chair. "What's going on?"

"I'll tell you while we get out of here. Just get your stuff."

"What about her?" Kid's head jerked in my direction.

Beard paused. He turned slowly to sneer at me. "What about her?"

My heart started again, pounding fast and hard. What about me? What were they going to do with me? All sorts of things flashed through my mind. Uppermost was the thought that I shouldn't have been so impatient for something to happen. Waiting in the kitchen and cooking was just fine with me. I didn't need anything to happen right then.

"Let's get rid of her. We can't leave her here to talk, and she'd be trouble to take with us," said Kid, running his finger over the blade of his knife. He caught me staring at him and slid the knife across his throat in a meaningful gesture. I gulped and tensed. I wasn't going to go down without a fight. Manny had taught us more than just how to break fingers. Still, I hated the thought of being cut up.

"She'll be trouble for sure, but we might need her. Besides, we don't have time to hide the body. She's coming with us. Boss's orders. We might be able to make her old man talk with her as a hostage. Come on." Beard headed for the garage door, pushing me ahead of him. I thought there really was sweat on his forehead. I knew there was on mine.

# Chapter Seven

"Okay, so the boss wants us to use the old lady here to make her husband give us what we want. I can buy that. But why is he in such an all-fired hurry all of a sudden?" Kid asked as Beard turned the van onto the freeway. Kid was seated in the middle of the second seat so he could keep an eye on me in the front passenger seat.

Beard didn't answer right away. He was busy concentrating on avoiding a car that had swerved in front of us. I saw him frown a little as he stepped on the brakes. The brakes. Of course, I hadn't had time to take the rope off. Didn't he remember putting the rope on? My brain froze for a minute then started going over the implications. Could it be he didn't know about the brakes? But if Beard didn't know, then . . . Then what? Had Kid put the ropes on without telling Beard? I glanced at Kid, who was waiting for Beard to answer his question. He hadn't seemed to notice Beard's reaction. What was going on?

"So? What's with the boss?" Kid asked.

"He's worried. He thinks the feds may be closing in on him, and he wants to make sure everything's right and tight on our end so he doesn't have to worry about things falling into the wrong hands. We have to find this Art guy by this evening or the boss will send bigger guns to do the job. He's jumpy as sin." Beard shook his head as if trying to rid himself of unpleasant thoughts.

Kid scrunched his eyebrows down in a frown. "That's not like the boss. He doesn't usually let anything get to him."

They were quiet for a few minutes while Beard steered the van along I-25. We passed the exit to Ft. Carson and kept going.

Clearing his throat, Kid said, "If you take the next exit, we could turn around and head south for El Paso. We could be there by tomorrow if we take turns driving, cross into Juarez, and just keep on going before anyone knew we were gone."

Beard gave a dry, little chuckle. "You're really something, kid."

"Yeah," agreed Kid.

The next exit flashed by.

"Hey! You missed the exit!" Kid protested.

"Yeah, you're really something," said Beard sarcastically. His voice increased in sarcasm as he continued. "You know what you are? You're stupid. Just what do you think would happen to us in Mexico? The boss isn't stuck in the States like the feds are. Part of his business is in Mexico, remember? He has contacts in Mexico, and some of them aren't very nice. Remember? You want to end up like some other people we used to know?"

"No," said Kid sullenly. Then he burst out, "I just think it's stupid to go looking for this guy when I already looked all over that place."

Beard sighed then spoke as if to a very young child. "If you hadn't noticed, today is much warmer than yesterday. Most of the snow that fell yesterday is off the lower mountains already. By the time we get up in the Florrisant area, most of the snow will be gone, and we'll be able to see a purple truck a mile away. So shut your trap, and let me do the driving."

Kid's face went an angry dark red, but he didn't say anything. He just settled back. We drove in silence for a few minutes. When it came time for Beard to slow down for the exit leading to Manitou Springs, I saw him frown again and glance down at the brake pedal. Were the brakes giving him trouble again? Why didn't Kid say anything? Was he mad enough at Beard to let us get killed? I knew why I didn't say anything. Right then I wanted to get into a crash. It would certainly solve a lot of my problems.

Unfortunately, the brakes held. We passed Manitou Springs. The freeway going up the canyon was wide, curving in gentle S-turns or remaining straight for miles, nothing too strenuous for the brakes. My ears needed popping, so I yawned. Then I yawned even wider, caught off guard by a sudden need for sleep. The warmth of the car and the gentle curves of the road were threatening to send me off, but I knew I couldn't fall asleep. So I struggled to stay awake. Kid yawned just after I did. Then Beard yawned too, proving that yawning is indeed contagious. I yawned again.

"Hey! Cut that out!" Kid shoved the point of his knife into my side.

I shut my mouth then had to stifle another yawn. It was harder than I thought it would be, but I managed. I didn't want Kid slicing me up. That wouldn't solve anything. The only way I wanted to die right then was if I could take Beard and Kid with me, but I didn't know if I could grab the steering wheel and hang on long enough to do any real damage if I was stabbed. I certainly didn't want them left around to hurt my family.

*NOTE: Professor Mallory, you don't have to worry that I'm harboring suicidal tendencies. I've talked to my psychiatrist, and he agrees it was a most natural reaction at the time for a mother to be willing to die in order to protect her children.*

By the time we got up to where the trees were close to the road, it was evident that most of the snow was indeed gone, but it was also evident that Beard had forgotten one thing: what happens when the snow melts—in other words, mud. Every road we passed leading to a campground was deeply rutted with mud. We even saw one road where a four-wheel-drive vehicle was up to its axles in mud, its tires spinning and spraying brown clods in all directions. Art would have stopped to help. A sudden wave of longing swept over me. All I wanted was to feel Art's arms around me. How I missed that man! How glad I was that he wasn't there right then. At least he was safe. He and the boys. I sent up a prayer of thanks.

"Have you ever gone camping up here?" Beard asked.

I blinked. Was he talking to me?

"You! You ever gone camping up here?" he nearly shouted at me.

"Yes," I answered.

"Where?"

"A little campground just off the road to Florrisant," I answered truthfully. Art never would have camped there, not if he wanted to go exploring instead of camping where other people would be.

"How far off the road?" Beard asked.

"We can't go off the road," Kid whined. "We'll get stuck in the mud."

Beard ignored him. "How far off the road?" he repeated grimly.

I shrugged. "About half a mile."

"OK," was all Beard said. A few minutes later, we were off the main road following Forest Service signs to the Florissant campgrounds. I could feel the tires slipping in the mud. There were no tire tracks on the road in front of us, though, so it wasn't too bad. Then Beard stopped the van. We weren't even close to the campground, so I wondered what in the world he was up to.

So did Kid. "What are you doing?"

"We're walking the rest of the way," Beard answered. "Come on. Get out."

"Are you crazy?" shouted Kid.

I watched with sudden interest as Beard got out of the van without paying the least bit of attention to me. He was arguing with Kid as he walked around to the side door of the van. Kid jumped out to argue back. I patted the set of keys in my pocket, just to make sure they were still there. I'd given Beard my spare set because I hadn't wanted him to know I had keys in my pocket ready to use if I got the chance. I thought I saw a chance right then. *Just let them take one step away from the van. Please, please, just one step.* Quietly, I slipped the keys out of my pocket and reached over to my door to gently push down the lock only to feel it stop halfway down. Then it popped back up as Beard yanked open my door and jerked me out of the van. I just had time to get the keys back into my pocket before I was all the way out.

It may have been warmer than usual for the end of May in the Rockies, but it was still cold. I wished Beard had given me time to get my jacket, but he'd seemed to be in a terrible hurry to get out of my house. A cool breeze sighed through the ponderosa pines, making the sun's promise of warmth into a lie. I could feel the goose bumps pop up.

"Which way to the campground you stayed at?" Beard asked.

After checking the Forest Service signs, I pointed at the trail toward the campground where we'd stayed the year before. I didn't bother to tell Beard that Art had called it a sissy camp because it had a fire pit and a cement pad. He'd only stayed there because the fire danger had been too high to have a fire in the back country and he'd been aching to go camping. Art hated camping anywhere you could hear your neighbors. I had to agree. There is something so restrictive about hearing other people laughing, arguing, singing, or whatever when you're out among the pines.

But I didn't have much time to reflect on Art's camping preferences because Beard gave me a shove in the direction of the trail. "Get going. No one's been out of here in a day or so. He might still be back there."

*Fat chance*, I thought. Slogging through the mud and leftover snow wasn't at all pleasant, especially in my running shoes with the mesh over the toes, but I went willingly enough—anything to keep these guys occupied and away from my family. Sister Luckendorf, our teacher in Relief Society, has a philosophy about teenage boys. She says that to keep them out of trouble you have to keep them upright and moving. I intended to use her philosophy on Beard and Kid. The more they were upright and moving, the better. If they wanted to hike, they were going to hike. I'd told them the campground was about half a mile back from the main road. It was actually nearer to two miles. Two miles is a long hike when your shoes weigh about ten pounds apiece from the caked mud. It's an even longer hike when you have a whiner dressed in black leather and chains tagging along behind, poking you with his knife just to let off steam from his bad temper. I know I felt that way, and from the way Beard kept glaring at his partner, I could tell he thought the same thing.

Even the cold and wind didn't stop me from noticing how beautiful it was up there. There were patches of snow striped with blue shadows from the leafless birches, and the sun was striking sparks where there were no shadows. It was too early in the year for bird sounds, but I could hear water running and dripping from the snow melting. I imagined Art and the boys enjoying just such a scene. I just hoped we didn't catch them enjoying it.

To my dismay, there was a tent at the campground and a dark-colored pickup, nearly hidden from our view, right behind it. As soon as I saw them, I stopped dead in my tracks. Beard nearly ploughed into me from behind. Kid stopped whining in mid-whine. We all stared as the tent flap moved. Then it was flung back by a mittened hand. A bundled-up figure stepped out and stared back at us.

"Hello, there," said the figure.

"Who's that, Roy?" called a feminine voice from inside the tent.

My breath came out in a huge sigh. Of course, I had known Art wouldn't be there, but it was so much better *knowing* Art wasn't there.

"Just some hikers," the bundled-up figure named Roy called back. Then to us he said, "You folks lost?" He tilted his head quizzically as he studied us. We must have looked even stranger to him than he did to us. At least he was dressed for the place. The only one of us who looked at all prepared was Beard, with his L.L.Bean jacket. Still, his Nike Air shoes were just as bad as mine for hiking in the mud and snow. Kid and I must have looked especially strange. I was dressed in only my bright yellow scout shirt, blue pants, and a thin jacket, and Kid looked even weirder with his black leather, chains, and dress boots caked with mud. I wondered what Roy thought of Beard's and Kid's matching bandaged little fingers.

"No, we're not lost," Beard finally spoke up. "Some friends of ours said they were going to be camping up here and invited us up for the day. Have you seen a purple Ford truck anywhere?"

Roy shook his head. "Nope. Haven't seen anyone since Saturday when the ranger checked in on us."

Beard raised his eyebrows. "How long have you been camping here?"

"'Bout two months." Roy shrugged. Then he chuckled. "Oh, we're not completely crazy. I've got a research grant from the government to do this."

Beard placed his hand on my arm, his chuckle an exact replica of Roy's. "I wasn't going to say anything about being crazy. Well, my friend here is shivering. We'd better get going. Good luck with your experiment or whatever." He raised his bandaged hand in a farewell gesture.

"Good luck finding your friends." Roy raised his hand as well.

We turned to leave, Beard's other hand tightening on my arm until it hurt. Did he think I would try to get Roy's help? I had more sense than to get a complete stranger hurt or killed. Besides, a stranger was just that, an unknown quantity. How did I know how Roy would react?

As we slogged back along the trail, I wondered what Beard was going to do now. There were lots of other campgrounds near Florissant. We couldn't possibly check out all of them. I was already feeling like my feet were suffering from frostbite, and I was sure Beard's feet must be as cold and wet as mine. It was all I could do to put one foot in front of the other. We'd been walking for some time before I realized that Kid hadn't whined or poked me once since we'd left Roy's campsite. At first, I was grateful for the silence and the peace. Then I started worrying about what he was up to. I could hear him squishing along behind me, but he wasn't making any other sound. That was good . . . or was it? But by then I was so miserably cold, I couldn't concentrate on anything else, let alone try to decide what Kid's behavior meant.

Kid still hadn't said a thing by the time we reached the van. He climbed into the middle seat, resuming his old place. I climbed back into the front passenger seat without a protest. The sun had warmed the van while we were gone, making the interior seem like a blessed sauna, and all I wanted to do was sit there soaking up the heat. Beard checked my seat belt to make sure it was on tight; then he went around the front of the van to the driver's side, climbed in, and started the engine.

As the engine roared to life, Kid blurted out, "We gotta go see the ranger!"

Beard's hand stopped in midair, reaching for the gear shift. He turned slowly in his seat to stare at Kid. I looked from Beard to Kid and back again. As amazing as it was, Kid had come up with an intelligent remark—though I didn't much like it. What if the ranger did know where Art and the boys were? To my dismay, Beard agreed.

"You're right. That's exactly where we need to go next." Beard nodded thoughtfully. "Do you know where the ranger station is?" he asked Kid.

"Yep. I passed one when I was up here yesterday, but it was closed because it was Sunday," Kid answered.

I prayed it would be closed today because it was a holiday, but no such luck. Unfortunately, I could see the station was open for business as we drove into the gravel parking lot about twenty minutes later. There was only one other car parked in front of the ranger station, which was unusual for a three-day weekend. Perhaps all the snow the day before had scared most of the campers away. That was too bad. If there weren't many campers, the rangers might be more likely to remember Art and the boys.

After parking to one side of the lot, just out of sight of the ranger station's windows, Beard said to Kid, "You watch her. I'll go in and ask."

Kid and I watched Beard enter the front door. As soon as the door shut behind the other man, Kid whined, "I wish he'd let us bring some of those cookies you made. I'm hungry."

That gave me an idea. "I hope the turkey's all right in the oven. It should be done in a couple of hours. I sure do like a nicely browned turkey with lots of gravy for the potatoes. The pies I made this morning should be cooled by now and just right to eat."

Kid brightened. "Yeah, you made pies, didn't you? There's still some ice cream left too."

I winced. My Häagan-Dazs. At the rate he'd been eating it, there were probably only two or three quarts left, hardly enough to be satisfying. But I'd even be willing to sacrifice my ice cream for my family, so I said, "There's nothing like ice cream and pie."

"Yeah," breathed Kid.

The door to the ranger station opened. I tensed. A man and a little boy came out, closely followed by Beard. His face was expressionless. What had he found out? I hated waiting, but I would hate worse to hear he'd found Art.

"So?" asked Kid as Beard climbed back into the van.

"Nothing," said Beard, and I felt the tension drain out of me, leaving me limp as a wet rag.

"Nothing?" repeated Kid.

"That's what I said!" Beard started the van with a roar, as if venting his frustration. But he didn't put it into gear. Instead, he pulled out his cell phone, punched in some numbers, listened, tried again. Angrily, he shoved the phone into his pocket. "Now the phone won't work. I'm supposed to call in to the boss."

I didn't tell him there were just some places in the mountains that were blind spots as far as reception. I wanted to let him think his phone was broken. Then I thought it might be better to tell him the truth, which might get us down out of the mountains and away from Art. I cleared my throat. "Cell phones don't work well in the mountains. You have to get down and away from them to make any calls."

Beard looked at me like I was some alien life-form and he couldn't quite figure out why I was helping him. But he put the van in gear and took the road leading back to Colorado Springs, saying a few things I shall not repeat. I'll just say they were highly uncomplimentary about cellular phone companies.

"Let's go back to the house. You know the phone works there," suggested Kid innocently, as if getting the phone to work was the only thought in his head. Actually, at that point, it probably was. I doubted he was capable of having two thoughts in there at once. Still, I knew he wanted to get back to the pie and ice cream. Beard just grunted.

We drove back in silence, with Beard pulling over every few miles to check the phone. It didn't work in the canyon either, but I could have told him that. If it didn't work high in the mountains, it wouldn't work when the mountains were towering over us. I was all for stopping though. The longer we were on the road, the better. As long we were driving, my family was safe.

# Chapter Eight

THE TURKEY WASN'T BURNED, BUT the roll dough was all over the kitchen counter by the time we got back to the house. With all the stops Beard had made, the trip down the mountain had taken twice as long as the trip up, so we didn't get back until it was just about the time I'd planned to have dinner in the first place. I decided to forget the rolls, but it gave Kid something else to complain about. He'd complained all the way back into Colorado Springs until Beard had finally agreed to go back to the house just to shut him up. The only time Kid was quiet was when we stepped back into the kitchen and were hit by the overwhelming smell of roast turkey. He just stood there breathing deeply and then went for the pie and ice cream.

Beard left me with Kid and checked out the house, presumably to make sure no one had come in while we were gone. No one had, but there were two phone messages, which Beard played back. The first one was from Jerry, Art's manager at the shop, just wanting to let me know everything was going fine and that I shouldn't worry about coming in. The second was from Kyle, telling me they had made better time than they'd thought they would and might be rolling into Colorado Springs sometime late tonight or perhaps the next morning. I was stunned. Kyle coming so soon? I hadn't had time to get rid of Beard and Kid yet.

My fingers working furiously to peel the potatoes were only a faint echo of how hard I was thinking. How could I get Beard and Kid out of the house without putting Art and the boys in danger? I didn't know if my plan would work that fast. Better yet, how could I get hold of the police so they could put Beard and Kid in jail, where they couldn't hurt anyone? I whacked the potatoes into quarters with a vengeance and tossed them into the pan of water. As I turned on the stove, I caught Beard looking at me consideringly. His steady staring unnerved me even more. What was he thinking?

I turned from him so he couldn't see my face and reached up into the cupboard for the salt to put in the potatoes, but I was so rattled I grabbed the box of herb tea next to it. I was about to put it back when a thought struck me with such force that when I think of it now, I'm sure it was a personal revelation in answer to my prayers.

*NOTE: Professor Mallory, Mormons believe in real answers to prayer. If you'd like to hear about how it works, just ask me. I'd be happy to talk to you about it.*

My fingers tightened on the box as I studied the words on it: "Sleepy Time Tea, Soothing Bedtime Refreshment." I'd bought the tea because in Relief Society we'd had a lesson

on ten helpful herbs for family use that went in conjunction
with a lesson the Sunday before on the Word of Wisdom.

*NOTE: Professor Mallory, I'd be happy to explain the
Word of Wisdom too. For now, all you need to understand
is that it says that herbs are for our benefit.*

Herbs are for our benefit. That struck a chord. I began to
smile and had to force my face into neutral, difficult though
that was. The possibilities were nearly making me giddy. I
had tried the tea once and then decided not to use it unless I
really needed it. It was not only soothing, it put me out like a
light. I didn't know if it would have the same effect on Beard
and Kid, but I was willing to give it a try. In fact, there were a
few other things I'd learned in Relief Society that might help
me carry out my plans. If they worked, Beard and Kid would
never know what hit them.

When I'd been lying on the floor the night before trying
to formulate some kind of plan, I'd been thinking along
similar lines but nothing as elegant as what I now had in
mind. The little sleep they had gotten would help and so
would the turkey dinner, but the Sleepy Time tea would help
even more. Making them sleepy was as far as I had gotten
with the plan before, but now I had to hide another smile. If
only nothing happened to upset things. If only Beard didn't
have some other wild idea about going someplace or sending
Kid off.

I don't own a teapot, so I had to boil water in a regular
pot for the tea bags to steep in, but that gave me another
idea. I tossed a couple of tea bags into the water with the
peas and in with the potatoes and also into the pan of water
and flour ready to make gravy. I added some powdered onion
and garlic to the peas and potatoes to disguise the flavor of

the tea. The tea to drink, however, I made triple strength. Kid had complained about not having coffee. I hoped he would accept the herb tea instead. Beard too. They probably drank coffee to keep themselves awake. Would they ever be surprised when the tea did just the opposite! I felt like King Limhi and the Nephites escaping from the Lamanites. I just hoped it worked as well.

When everything was ready, Beard and Kid were only too willing to sit down to eat. I was amazed that Kid wanted anything after the way he'd filled himself with pie and ice cream, but he made happy, little smacking noises—which I would normally have found annoying to the extreme—as he surveyed the feast I'd laid out. As it was, I was pleased he still felt he could eat.

Kid picked up his tea cup filled with steaming brown liquid. "What's this? I thought you said you didn't have any coffee?"

"It's tea," I said.

He sniffed at it. "It doesn't smell like tea."

"Herbal tea," I said. I was beginning to get nervous. Why did he have to make such a fuss? "You said you wished you could have coffee, and that's as near as I could come. Do you want cream and sugar?" I didn't know much about how people like to drink coffee, except I had a vague idea that cream and sugar somehow went with it. How much or how little was and is still a complete mystery.

"Herbal tea! Ha!" Kid set his cup down with a disparaging clank.

Unexpectedly, Beard saved the day. "I want cream and sugar with mine. At least it's something hot to drink, and I could sure use it."

"It's real cream," I said encouragingly as I got out the carton of old-fashioned, extra-heavy cream I'd bought to whip to go with my ice cream and some homemade fudge sauce.

"Oh, all right. Where's the sugar?" Kid said as he took the cream from me.

From there on, getting them to take in as much Sleepy Time tea as possible was a piece of cake, or should I say, pie, since that was what was for dessert. The only problem was that it didn't seem to affect them at all. I kept waiting for their eyelids to get droopy or for a yawn or two, but nothing happened. I couldn't understand it. They'd had no more than three hours of sleep the night before, and not much before that either. They were full of a wonderful turkey dinner, which was full of enough carbohydrates to make any dinner guest ready for a good nap, but they seemed as alert as ever. What had I done wrong? According to a lesson we'd had about what kinds of foods to eat at different times of the day, I'd given those two men exactly what was *not* the kind of meal to eat if you wanted to stay awake.

While I was clearing away dishes and pondering the matter, the phone rang. At first I thought it was my phone, but then I realized it was Beard's cellular. He got up from the table and went into the family room, where he stood facing Kid and me, listening. Beard's expression changed to one of surprise and then quickly back to normal. He answered only a few words and then put the phone in his shirt pocket. Both Kid and I watched as he came back into the kitchen. He stopped in front of us, his arms folded across his chest as he announced, "The boss is sending someone to help resolve this little problem. They're on the plane now and should be arriving in Colorado Springs in about two hours. Give them an hour to get their luggage, rent a car, and make it here, and that means we should be seeing them here at about"—he looked at his watch—"ten o'clock."

I couldn't believe what I was hearing. More gangsters? How was I going to deal with more gangsters?

"What? What can anyone else do? We just have to wait until the dad and boys come back. Is the boss mad?" asked Kid. For the first time, I heard something sounding like fear in his voice.

Beard sneered. "Scared?"

"You shut up! I never been scared in my life." Kid shook his fist at Beard.

"Relax. As soon as those guys get here, we're free of this case. The boss needs our help back at headquarters. The feds are closing in, and he needs us there because we know what's going on. The new guys will just babysit here until the rest of the family comes home and the guys can get what we came for. OK?" Beard sauntered into the family room and sank into the easy chair. He flicked on the television with the remote, seemingly without a care in the world.

Kid's shoulders eased lower. I could tell he'd been tense no matter what he'd said about never being scared. He glanced at me, and I saw his face darken. "You, old woman, get this stuff cleaned up. You're going to have more guests!" he snarled. He seemed angry that I'd seen him frightened. Glancing around the room, his gaze lit on a family picture. He grabbed it from the wall, broke the glass with the butt of his knife, and stabbed at the picture over and over again—first Art, then me, then the boys and Veronica. Finally, he drew the knife deliberately through my three little granddaughters, watching my face all the time as he separated their heads from their bodies. I felt bile rising up in my throat at the viciousness of the act. When Kid saw me raise the back of my hand to press it against my mouth, he let out some of those hateful "heh, heh, heh" laughs.

"I said clean this place up!" he spat out.

I nodded, picking up plates and utensils as best I could with shaking hands. He was a beast, and Beard was no better. He just sat there and watched the whole thing.

Cleaning up had been part of the plan to keep me awake, but that was before my captors' adrenalin had started pumping. Would they ever fall asleep? Beard yawned. I glanced at him sharply. He ran his good hand over his eyes and chin then pushed the recliner back. Maybe my plan wasn't a total loss. I looked at Kid. He sat at the table, digging designs into it with the point of his knife. There was no sign of tiredness. Oh well. I could always hope. Meanwhile, it was time to put the rest of my plan into action.

I pulled a bucket and a mop out of the broom closet and set them by the sink. Then I filled the bucket with hot water. When I picked up the dishwashing liquid and squirted some in, I noticed the warning label. On the back of the bottle were the little words, "Do not mix with chlorine bleach." I smiled, reaching for the little bottle of bleach I had under the sink. Once the entire bottle of bleach was mixed in, unpleasant fumes started rising. I grabbed a bottle of ammonia and added some of that to the mixture as well. Sister Hobson's lesson on what household cleansers not to mix was coming in handy. The stench was nearly unbelievable, but those guys deserved every whiff they breathed in. I had to hold my breath as I carried the bucket over to the edge of the kitchen floor where it met the family room carpet, which happened to be right behind the couch. On my way there, I nearly bumped into Kid, who passed me without a word and plopped himself onto the couch, yawning largely. Beard shook his head and rubbed his eyes again. Kid didn't even try to fight off his fatigue. He just laid his head back against the couch and stared at the television, his eyelids drooping lower and lower.

Satisfied, I went back to the kitchen sink. The fumes were far enough away that I could just barely smell them. I didn't know if they would do any good making Beard and Kid sleepy, but I felt the fumes might make the two men sick if nothing else. It was worth a try, and that picture-cutting episode had made me angry enough to want to harm them.

Back at the sink, I turned on the water full force and just let it run while I moved dishes from the table to the counter, making as much noise as possible. After one particularly loud clank, I glanced at the two men to see if they'd noticed, but they hadn't stirred. Hm. Maybe it was time to start phase two of my plan. I went into the bathroom and got the superglue out of the drawer. It was hard as a rock. Oh well. I'd planned on gluing the door to the bathroom shut and leaving the water on just to make it harder for them to figure out I wasn't in there. It was probably a dumb idea anyway.

Instead, I took out the sliding part of the bathroom window and set it down in the tub, along with the screen. At least it might look like I'd gone out the window. I just hoped they wouldn't think I was too fat to make it. After turning on the water in the sink, I carefully locked the door and slid back into the kitchen, quietly closing the bathroom door behind me. I stood there for a moment, contemplating Beard and Kid. Both of them appeared to be sound asleep. Now what?

My stomach tensed as I tried to decide what to do next. Did I dare make a run for the van? Beard's car was still parked a block away. I thought of taking Beard's car keys so the men couldn't follow me, but the keys were in his pants pocket and I didn't want to risk waking him up. Chewing on my lower lip, I debated the pros and cons of going for the van or running down the street to the bus stop. On the one hand, there was the noise of the garage door opening, and on the other, I had no idea when the next bus was coming. Either way, I had to make it to Memorial Park, where most of the police force was going to be gathered tonight, including Manny.

Above the sound of water running into the kitchen sink, I became aware of a gentle snoring coming from Beard. That decided me. I grabbed my purse from the counter and went out into the garage, being careful to close the kitchen door ever so quietly.

The van keys were still in my pocket, for which I was eternally grateful. In my mind's eye I had visions of Hollywood-style fumbling in my purse with shaking hands and keys falling to the concrete floor of the garage while I scrabbled around on my hands and knees trying to find them. My hands shook all right, but I managed to climb into the van and insert the keys smoothly into the ignition, congratulating myself on how coolly I was behaving. Then things started to go wrong.

# Chapter Nine

First, I closed the van door out of habit, forgetting how loud it could slam. Not only did the door slam loudly, it slammed on the seat belt and popped open again. My heart dropped into my stomach and then leaped up, lodging in my throat. I expected the kitchen door to open any second, revealing a gun-toting Beard or the kid.

Grabbing for the garage door opener with one hand, I turned the key with the other and then pulled the van door shut again. The garage door was still going up. I could hardly wait for it. Only the fear of the loud noise it would make kept me from smashing through it. Then the door stopped and started down again like it does when one of the links in the chain gets kinked. Of all the times to do something like that! I hit the steering wheel with the heel of one hand while pressing the opener again with the other. The door started back up, but it was still agonizingly slow. *Oh, please don't let those men wake up*, I prayed, nearly jumping out of my skin

I was so scared. Gunning the engine, I quickly backed out of the garage, changing my prayer to one of thanksgiving that Beard and Kid hadn't shown up. Too soon. The front door burst open just as I started forward. Beard and Kid ran out onto the front lawn, took one look at me and the van heading down the street, and ran down the block to Beard's car.

I stepped on the gas, hoping against all hope that no little kids would run into the street. This was a residential area. I could kill someone going this fast. Beard or Kid could kill me. I stepped on the gas pedal harder, making my top-heavy vehicle lean dangerously around a turn. One more turn to the right and I was out of the subdivision, racing down the hill to the highway connecting us to the rest of Colorado Springs. I looked in the rearview mirror. The sight of Beard's car turning out of the subdivision put more fear into my heart than I'd ever thought possible. If this was the way rabbits felt when they were chased by dogs, I wondered why they didn't just drop dead on the spot. The needle on the speedometer climbed from fifty to seventy.

Luckily there weren't many cars on the road. Everyone was probably already at Memorial Park listening to the Colorado Springs Symphony playing the pieces leading up to their grand finale when it turned dark—the "1812 Overture" complete with artillery from Ft. Carson and fireworks overhead timed to go off with the artillery blasts. It was a spectacular experience. I only wished I was there right then, enjoying myself with Angela and the kids.

I glanced in the mirror again only to find that Beard's car was closer and gaining fast. Didn't the man have any nerves? He must have been going at least a hundred. At this rate he'd catch up to me in seconds. I became a little calmer when I asked myself what Beard could possibly do if he did catch up.

My van was much bigger than his little car. He'd be toast if he tried to run into me. I've always believed the line from *Don Quixote*: "Whether the pot hits the rock or the rock hits the pot, it's going to be bad for the pot." Beard was driving a pot. I was driving a rock.

Another glance in the mirror showed me Beard was only a hundred feet or so behind me. Steady, I told myself. I hung onto the steering wheel so it wouldn't pull out of my hands if Beard tried to run me off the road. Crash! An explosion behind me shocked me into jerking the wheel, and I realized Beard had shot out the rear window of the van. Splinters of glass flew against the dashboard. One shard grazed my right arm, leaving it stinging, but nothing else hit me. The seat and headrest, or maybe my guardian angel, must have shielded me. I prefer to think it was my guardian angel since the next thing I knew, my right foot was pumping the spongy brake pedal while my hands wrestled the steering wheel to turn the car into the little subdivision clustered next to the entrance on to the highway. While the van rocked wildly, I saw Beard's car shoot past on the main road. I knew I only had a head start when I heard the squealing of his tires. He was trying to turn back in my direction.

The one advantage I had over Beard was how well I knew the area, which was hardly any advantage at all. I rarely drove through this neighborhood since the main road connected with the highway. One of Evan's friends had lived somewhere in here, and I'd driven the boy home once about three years ago, which wasn't much help. I thought there was a way through the subdivision and onto the highway, if only I could remember it. I turned right at the next corner. Yes, this looked familiar. Then I turned left and left again, only to face a Dead End sign and a cul-de-sac. Turning around on the cul-de-sac, I prayed I wouldn't run right into Beard and Kid. Stopping at the next corner, I peered up and down the empty street. No sign of Beard's car, thank goodness. Five minutes later I was driving down the highway, heaving huge sighs of relief. Now to get to Memorial Park and Manny, or any other policeman, so they could set up some kind of protection around my house before Kyle and Veronica and the girls got there.

The closer to Memorial Park I got, the heavier the traffic became. It seemed like everyone in the Springs was going to the big event, which was all right with me. The more people, the less likely it was that Beard and Kid would start shooting again. I kept looking in my rearview mirror through the broken glass of the back window for any sign of the thugs, but I didn't see them. My hands were sweating so badly, I worried I wouldn't be able to hang on to the steering wheel if I had to do any more fancy driving.

Once I was off the highway and onto the city streets, traffic was even worse. The cars around me slowed to a crawl and then a standstill as we turned into the main parking lot near the park. There was usually a policeman at the entrance to the parking areas for the Memorial Day event, but I couldn't see an officer. The music was well under way, though, so it was possible most of the policemen were nearer to the music. I squinted as I searched through the gathering dusk. The scene before me was surreal under the glare of lights making the shadows black. Then, as I turned my head, I caught a glimpse of the reflection in my rearview mirror and went into shock. Beard's car was only two cars back. How he got there was a mystery to me. I could have sworn I'd lost him for good. My search for a policeman became frantic, but there were none to be found. I started hyperventilating. Beard and Kid were probably just waiting to see where I was going before they jumped out and grabbed me. Well, I wasn't going to wait around to be kidnapped again.

When the cars ahead of me crept forward and to the right a little, I realized no one in Beard's car could see the left side of my van. Remembering to turn off the overhead light that goes on when the door opens, I opened the van door just enough to slide down and out. No more stupidity for me. At least, I hoped not. I hunkered down, slipping between parked cars until I reached some tall bushes that hid me from view of people in the parking lot. There were people everywhere, all heading toward the music coming from the center of the park. The glaring lights were still on, and the orchestra was playing a Souza march. That meant they hadn't quite reached the finale, which was good and bad. It was bad because Beard or Kid could see me more easily, especially in my bright yellow Scout shirt with the tomato stain that looked like blood. It was good because, with the lights on, I'd have an easier time trying to find Manny.

I started to run toward the music, dodging into and out of the shadows of the trees, bushes, and shrubs peppering the park, hoping Beard and Kid wouldn't be able to see me. I hate running. When I run, the fat on my back jiggles. Other parts of me jiggle too, but for some reason, my back jiggling is what bothers me the most. Besides, I can only run short distances before I feel like I'm going to faint. Then I jiggle and gasp, calling attention to just how idiotic I look. But right then, my back jiggling and my loud gasping barely got a passing thought. All I could think of was getting away from Beard and Kid and finding Manny.

The march came to an end just as I reached the area where people had laid out blankets and picnic goodies. Somewhere in there were Angela and her children, and somewhere around the edges of the crowd would be Manny. A man stepped out of the shadows just ahead of me, and I nearly had a heart attack until I realized it wasn't Beard or Kid. I dodged a teenager throwing firecrackers. Manny would have loved to throttle him. Any other time, I'd have done it myself. Anyone who throws firecrackers in a crowd is abysmally stupid and deserves to be throttled, thereby depleting the stupidity gene pool for all of humanity. I dodged another kid throwing grapes at people, and then I nearly got hit by a Frisbee as I skirted the stands of bushes placed around the park, working my way closer and closer to where the symphony was seated under a large pavilion. I could just see several uniformed figures standing on either side of the pavilion. Scanning the grounds behind me, I could also see two men jogging purposefully in my direction. I couldn't tell for sure, but they looked like Beard and Kid. I felt like lying down and giving up, but some inner strength pushed me on. Panting painfully rasping breaths, I tried to make my shaking legs go faster. Several people looked at me strangely, probably wondering what an overweight woman with blood on her Scout shirt was doing trying to run. No one offered to help though. They just looked irritated that I was intruding on their evening.

"And now, ladies and gentlemen, the event you've all been waiting for. The Colorado Springs Symphony plays the '1812 Overture!'" the announcer exclaimed to deafening cheers as the lights went out, leaving the park in darkness. I had to stand still for a moment to get my night vision; then I began running again—stumbling is more like it—trying to step on as few people as possible. At least, if I couldn't see anyone, Beard and Kid would have trouble finding me. But even though I'd seen them behind me, I kept expecting them to jump out from every shrub or bush I passed.

Closer to the pavilion, the music was deafening. The symphony orchestra had microphones in front of them, and their concert was being blasted through six-foot-high speakers placed at either end of the pavilion. There were several men in uniform walking around, but I couldn't tell if they were soldiers getting the cannons ready or policemen. I know anyone interested in military things could probably tell the difference in less light than there was that night, but I sure couldn't. I could tell the ones in fatigues or BDUs or whatever they're called now. But the dress uniforms were harder to tell apart from police uniforms. In the dark, uniforms are uniforms are uniforms.

By then I was gasping for breath so badly, I couldn't even stop one of them and ask which one they were or if they knew Manny. Besides, I was afraid and confused, and each shadowy man reminded me of Beard or Kid, as ridiculous as I knew that to be.

How was I going to find Manny? "Manny?" I whispered between gasps. "Manny? Where are you?" I could feel tears running down my face. To get so close and not be able to find him filled me with despair and terror. Breathing as deeply as I could, I shouted hoarsely, "Manny?" just as the music hit that quiet part of the overture just before it gets really loud. Some of the people on blankets shushed me. "Manny?" I repeated over and over as I stumbled through the darkness.

The music intensified, but I was too distressed to notice until the cannons went off, startling me terribly. Then an all-too-familiar grasp on my shoulder made me scream, just as the second cannon went off. Fear ignited me. I grabbed the hand grasping my shoulder, found the little finger and yanked it as hard as I could as I gathered the strength to run. It was only when the owner of the hand yelled, "Jane!" that I collapsed into a heap on the grass, laughing and sobbing at the same time. The hand belonged to Manny—the same Manny I'd been looking for, the same Manny who had taught me how to break fingers. My home teacher. I leaned against his legs and laughed and sobbed until I was weak, listening to Manny bite off words he probably hadn't said since he was baptized. Garbage can words or not, they sounded awfully good to me.

When he was through shaking his hand and trying not to cuss, Manny dropped to the grass beside me as the cannons went off again. "Geez Louise, Jane, why did you have to do that?" he hissed in my ear when it was just music again, albeit loud music. I have to hand it to the Colorado Springs Symphony—they're really enthusiastic about the "1812 Overture."

I flinched as another cannon went off. In the light of the fireworks, I saw Manny look more closely at my face and then down at my stained Cub Scout shirt. He reached up with his good hand to brush at the tears on my cheeks. "Hey. You're crying. Are you hurt? What's going on?"

"I'm not hurt. I was kidnapped," I managed before it was time for the cannons again.

"What?" Manny's voice sounded shocked. He stood and reached down his good hand to help me up. "Let's get away from the music so we can talk." He led me toward a police car parked behind some shrubs, cradling his broken finger against his chest as he walked. When we were inside the car with the doors and windows shut, he said, "Tell me." Then he handed me his handkerchief.

"Your hand," I protested, blowing my nose and wiping my eyes. "Let's get that fixed first. I'm so sorry, Manny. I thought you were Beard or Kid."

"Never mind about my hand. Who are Beard and Kid? What's going on?" he demanded.

"They're after Art or something Art has," I said. Then, as quickly as possible, I explained about what had happened. The music and big guns continued, and the light from the fireworks flashed sporadically, lighting up the interior of the car. In spite of the weirdness of the setting, I felt safer than I had since Saturday. Blessedly safe. When I was finished, I said, "I don't know what they want or where it is or why they want it. I just know they believe Art is the key to finding it, and they're willing to do anything to get it. From what they've said, other members of their organization have killed or been killed, and I can tell they're pretty dangerous themselves."

"They shot at you, didn't they? I'd say that's pretty dangerous," Manny huffed, squinting at the brightness of another burst of fireworks.

"Not only that, but two more of them are on the way to my house right now. What if Kyle and Veronica and the girls show up at the same time?" I started to shake again at the thought of my dear ones in the clutches of men like Beard and Kid.

Manny sat quietly for a moment. Then he took the mike of the car radio and spoke into it. After the preliminaries, he said to the dispatcher, "Listen, Carla. I've got a tip that two hit men are headed for 6975 Sullivan. Send a patrol car there to wait for them. Advise extreme caution. They're probably armed." After signing off, he turned to me. "You say you saw your kidnappers in the park? Are you up to coming with me for a few minutes? I need to tell the sergeant."

I nodded slowly. I felt so safe in the police car; I hated to leave it, but I didn't want to be left there without Manny either. My legs felt rubbery as I climbed out of the car and let him shepherd me over to where some shadowy figures were standing at one end of the pavilion. One of the figures left the others and came toward us.

The overture was over, so the symphony was playing things like the themes to *Star Wars* and *Superman* and other pieces that lent themselves to fireworks displays. At any other time, I would have enjoyed it immensely. As it was, all I could think was that somewhere out there were two men who had tried to kill me.

Manny greeted the shadowy figure. "Hi, Sarge. We've got a situation here."

The sergeant led us around to the back of the pavilion where we could talk. When he'd been told the whole story and made sure I was all right, he stood there stroking his chin. "It seems to me," he said, "that the first thing we need to do is capture the two kidnappers, but in this crowd it will be next to impossible to find them."

I had told myself earlier that I was through with stupidity, but the very next thing I said disproved that theory big time. The only sane reason I can think as to why I did it is that I wanted Beard and Kid captured and put as far away from my family as possible. Before I could stop myself, I offered, "Why don't we go back to my van, and I'll act like I'm having trouble starting it. Beard and Kid will probably show up, and you can grab them." As soon as the words were out of my mouth, I felt like washing it out with soap. Especially when the sergeant liked the idea. The next thing I knew, Manny and the sergeant had given some of the other officers instructions, and I was being escorted around the perimeter of the darkened park, with Manny walking several feet behind me and staying in the shadows as much as possible. The others had gone off in different directions. Even with Manny there, I felt terribly vulnerable.

We were nearly to the parking lot when the fireworks and music stopped. The lights came on all over the park. People were picking up blankets and leftover food and wandering back to the parking lot. I could hear cars starting and saw through the stands of bushes and trees that a line was already forming to leave. My stomach churned more and more the closer we got. I had to keep reminding myself that there would be several policemen watching over me and that I would be just fine, but the thought of coming anywhere near Beard or Kid gave me major heartburn.

"This is as far as I go. Will you be all right?" Manny said from the shadow of a clump of shrubs and trees.

"What? Oh, sure," I said, pulled out of my worries by the sound of his voice. I took a deep breath to steady myself then continued on toward the van. I decided that if I hadn't found Manny, I wouldn't just walk up to the van without a care in the world, so I hurried from bush to bush, peering around them as if on the lookout for Beard and Kid, which I was. In one clump, I actually bumped into one of the police officers, nearly screaming until I realized it wasn't either Beard or Kid. I backed out again in a hurry. The officer only grinned at me and gave me the OK sign before slipping deeper into the shadows, where he was invisible. The harshly bright lighting made the shadows especially black. I just hoped I didn't bump into Beard or Kid the same way, but by then I was pretty close to where I'd left the van. I gulped for air as I slipped to the next clump of bushes and the next.

When I'd left the van so abruptly, I'd left it blocking traffic. For the first time, I thought about what a mess I'd probably caused. But as I approached, I saw that with everyone trying to leave, the van was sitting by itself in the incoming lane, and the traffic was flowing around it fairly smoothly.

An awful thought occurred to me. What if Beard and Kid were hiding *in* the van? I didn't want to climb into the van just to have Beard or Kid rise up from the backseat and point that gun at me or slit my throat, so I cautiously peered in the shattered back window and the side windows before opening the driver's door and heaving myself up into the seat.

One of the oddest parts of the whole thing was that I still had my purse with the car keys in it. Habit is strong, I've decided, especially in women who carry purses. Taking the keys out of my purse, I tried to insert them into the ignition, but my hands were shaking so hard, I did the Hollywood thing and dropped them. For a moment I just stared at them lying on the floor amid shards of glass. I hoped Beard and Kid were watching. That was an especially convincing move, even if I didn't mean it to be. I gingerly picked the keys up, careful not to cut myself on the glass, and got them into the ignition. Usually the van roars into life the instant the key is turned, so I had to wiggle the key off and on to make it start and die quickly. It sounded pretty realistic, if I say so myself. I tried it again, willing myself not to look up for fear of spooking Beard and Kid. Where were they? Where were the policemen? I felt like crying again. Why had I been so quick to play decoy? I started and killed the engine a third time, then a fourth, wanting nothing more than to let it roar to life and take off as fast as I could.

Shouts. Something slammed up against the van, rocking it. More shouts. I twisted in the seat, craning my neck around to my right so I could see whatever had hit the van. Kid's face was pressed up against the glass, his hands spread-eagled on either side of his head, the bandage on his little finger gleaming bright white in the lights, and the blade of the knife glinting wickedly from his other hand. A police officer's face was just visible behind him.

Kid's eyes met mine malevolently. I'd never been the object of so much hate in my life. I knew right then he would have killed me if he could have gotten his hands on me. Shivering, I slid from the van to try to find Manny among the crowd of police officers milling around. He was standing over Beard, who was face down on the road. Manny's service revolver was pointed at Beard's head. "Just try to move," Manny barked in a voice that said he was wishing the man would try. I'd never heard Manny so angry before. It gave me a whole new perspective on my home teacher.

# Chapter Ten

I'D NEVER BEEN TO A police station and watched people being booked before. I was a little disappointed to find out it was very much like the way they show it on television, only not as dramatic. No one cried. No one had hysterics. Kid did cuss at me a little, but the officers took him into another room. They hurried Beard away pretty fast too, but not so fast that quite a few officers didn't have time to notice and comment on three identically broken fingers. Manny's had been bandaged by then. I gained an instant reputation—as what, I wasn't quite sure, but some of the officers seemed to think it was pretty funny.

The biggest relief came when the sergeant got a phone call from the officers who had gone to my house. His face broke into a big grin as he listened. I wanted to hear, and Manny must have wanted to as well because he started to ask the sergeant something. But the man just waved Manny back and continued to talk and listen for a little while longer.

I felt like shaking him; I wanted to know so badly what had gone on.

"So what happened?" Manny asked as soon as the sergeant hung up.

The sergeant chuckled, shaking his head. "It was too easy. McKinney and Strate in one car and Roberts and Greerson in another got to the house minutes after the dispatcher called them. Jane, here, had left the garage door open, so they drove both of their cars in and shut the door. Then they went inside and waited. Sure enough, the two guys showed up a few minutes ago and just walked in. They didn't knock or anything. All four officers were waiting for them, weapons drawn and trained right on them. No contest. The men gave up without a struggle. McKinney and Strate are bringing them in right now. They were calling from their car."

I sank down into a nearby chair, letting out gusty sigh after gusty sigh. I didn't know whether to laugh or cry or what. I cried. The sergeant made up for making me wait by handing me his handkerchief.

"Oh, by the way, Jane. Your son and his wife and kids drove up to the house just as the officers were taking walking those guys out to the car. Were you expecting them? I told McKinney and Strate to have Roberts and Greerson stay at the house until further notice just in case anyone else shows up," the sergeant added.

Kyle and Veronica and the girls! What if they'd shown up just a few minutes earlier? I shuddered to think about what could have happened. I shut my eyes for a minute and sent up a silent prayer of thanks that my family was safe.

"Why don't I drive Jane home? She's had a long couple of days," Manny suggested, and the sergeant nodded.

"What about my van?" I asked.

"We'll need it for evidence for a few days," the sergeant said. "We'll take pictures of the shot-out window, try to find the slug, dust for fingerprints. You know, that kind of stuff. We'd like to get the first two on attempted homicide as well as kidnapping. The other two we'll have to see about. Breaking and entering is about all we can do for the time being. Hopefully they'll all be wanted for other things as well."

I shrugged. "OK. Anything to keep them put away as long as possible." But I wondered what I was going to do without my van for a while.

The ride home seemed to take forever. The events of the past two days kept repeating over and over again in my mind—the slapped cheek, that knife, cooking, being tied up, cooking, that knife, tromping through the mud, cooking, even the way Beard and Kid had looked leaping up when the television had blared out the national anthem. I hadn't told Manny that part, so I told him then, and he laughed so hard he had to wipe his eyes with his bandaged hand (I felt so bad about breaking his finger). I laughed a little too, and the laughter seemed to ease some of the tightness around my heart.

"Jane, you are something else. Are you sure you don't want to join the police force or even the FBI? Maybe the CIA? They could use someone like you. Spies wouldn't stand a chance," Manny chuckled.

"No, thank you. I've had enough adventure to last me a lifetime. The only thing I ask is that you back me up when I tell Art what happened. He's not going to believe it. He'll probably think I made the whole thing up to explain why the back window on the van is broken," I joked.

"Just show him your black eye, and he'll believe you."

"What black eye?" I put my hands up to feel both of my eyes. The left one did feel a little puffy and sore. So much had happened, I hadn't noticed until then.

"Didn't you know you have a shiner? What did they do, hit you?" Manny's voice was sounding angry again. It was kind of nice knowing he felt protective toward me.

"It must have been from when Beard slapped me. I tried to answer the phone," I explained. Manny grunted. I went on, "You know, it sounds funny to keep calling them Beard and Kid. Do you know what their names are?"

Manny shook his head. "No, they wouldn't talk. Neither would the other two. Don't worry. We took their fingerprints. Guys like that will have a record somewhere, and we'll find out who they are."

"I just keep wondering why they were after Art?"

"So do I," said Manny grimly.

When Manny and I finally made it into my house, I was met by a tornado of little girls and questions. I hugged my granddaughters so tight they squealed, but I couldn't help myself, nor could I help the tears that slipped down my cheeks because I was so thankful they were safe. Kyle enveloped me in a huge bear hug.

Kyle was the first to ask. "I was in shock when I saw those policemen escorting those guys out of the house. What's been going on, Mom? Dad can't leave you alone for more than a few hours, and look at the mess you get yourself into," he teased, but I could see the concern on his face.

"Kyle!" protested Veronica. She raised her eyebrow at me, and we exchanged glances that said we both knew Kyle was the biggest tease in the universe. She smiled at her husband. "It's time I took these little ones off to bed." She gathered her protesting children and herded them to the back of the house. I wondered which room she'd chosen to put them in since I hadn't been able to get anything ready. Oh well. She seemed to have figured something out.

"It's more like look at the mess your mom got your dad out of," said Manny. "Those guys were really after your father."

"Dad? What do they want with Dad?" Kyle looked shocked.

I shrugged. "We still don't know. But the police are trying to find out. We'll have to be patient for now. I'm just glad your father is safe."

"Gee, I can't trust my own folks to stay out of trouble. It looks like I'll have to accept that transfer and promotion my company offered me to move here to the Springs just to take care of them." Kyle grinned at Manny then at me.

My eyes opened wide. "Really, truly? You're moving back here where I can see you and Veronica and my grandbabies all the time?" I burst into tears.

Kyle gathered me back into his arms. "I didn't think you'd take it so hard, Mom. If you'd rather we didn't come, we can always stay in Texas."

I punched him.

"Okay, okay. Does that mean you wouldn't mind watching the girls for a while after the graduation celebration so we can look for a house?" Kyle asked.

I just laughed weakly, resting my cheek against his chest. It would have been nice to be doing that to Art, but Kyle was a good substitute for Art right then.

The doorbell rang, and one of the policemen—Greerson, according to his name tag—went to answer it. Excited female voices reached me, then Mary Ann and Carline, my visiting teachers, burst into the living room. I looked at Manny, puzzled about how they knew to come. He pantomimed calling on the phone. Dear man to think of how much I'd need my visiting teachers.

"Are you all right?" Mary Ann asked.

"Where did you get that black eye?" asked Carline.

"Black eye?" growled Kyle. He held me away from him to take a good look at my face. "Did they do that to you?"

"It wasn't Manny," I quipped.

"No, but she did this to me." Manny held up his bandaged finger.

"Well, you taught me how in Relief Society," I said.

"So it's my fault?" Manny answered back.

Carline chuckled. "I remember that lesson, but I never thought I'd have to use it. Jane, I want to hear the whole story."

"Me too," said Mary Ann.

"We do too," joined in Veronica, who'd just walked back into the room.

"We do too," said Roberts and Greerson.

I yawned. "It's nearly midnight. I'm dying to take a shower and get in my own bed, but I promise I'll tell you everything tomorrow."

They all looked disappointed, especially the two police officers.

"OK, but when we come back to hear your story, can we count it as a visiting teaching visit? It's nearly the end of the month," asked Mary Ann.

Roberts and Greerson just stared at the rest of us when we burst out laughing.

I thought I'd have trouble sleeping because of nightmares or something worse, but I slept like a log. Maybe it was knowing that Roberts and Greerson and then their replacements were watching over me during the night and that Kyle and Veronica and their children were all safe. Whatever it was, I didn't wake up until ten the next morning, and then I only woke up because two grandchildren were bouncing on my bed.

"Hey!" I yelped when a little body landed on my stomach.

The two little girls scrambled off the bed and raced for the door. Tessa, the oldest, shouted, "Mommy, Grandma's awake!"

I just shook my head and got up, moaning at my sore muscles. I caught sight of myself in the mirror over the dresser and stared. I did have a black eye, and where my nightgown's short sleeves ended, I could see huge bruises where the cords had bitten into my arms and where Beard and Kid had grabbed me. Lovely. My hair was sticking up all over too. I'd gone to bed with wet hair after my shower, too tired to dry it. Well, another shower would fix that. Grabbing my robe, I started for the connecting bathroom, but there was a knock on the bedroom door.

"Yes?" I said, gathering the robe around me as I opened the door.

Veronica was standing there. "Sorry to bother you, but Manny called and said that when you woke up they want you over at the police station to make a statement."

I sighed. I guessed I hadn't heard the last of this thing and would go on hearing about it for a long time. "OK. Just let me get cleaned up and get something to eat. Is he coming here? They still have my van."

"I'm supposed to call and let him know when you'll be ready. Should I tell him to be here in an hour?" Veronica asked.

"Sure," I answered, and then I went to take that shower.

Manny showed up right on time, so he had to wait for me a little while. I'm afraid I wasn't too anxious to get back to the police station. On the way, Manny dropped a bombshell, "We found out who all of those guys are."

"Really?" I turned in my seat to stare at him. "Who? And don't tell me they have nice normal names. I want them to be Big Tony or Crusher the Avenger or some other colorful gangster-type name."

Manny laughed. "Sorry to disappoint you. The one you called Kid is really James McIntire. That's a nice, normal name. On the other hand, he does have a record that would make you proud. He's known to have killed at least four people, but he's always evaded the cops. If it hadn't been for you, he'd still be free."

I shuddered. I'd known Kid—or James McIntire—was capable of killing. There was something evil about him that I couldn't help noticing. And I'd calmly baked cookies for him. I shuddered again. "What about Beard?" I asked.

"You won't believe me when I tell you," said Manny.

"Won't believe what?"

"What we found out about him."

"Tell me. I'll believe."

"I don't know if you can take it," Manny answered.

I groaned. "Quit stalling and just tell me or I'll break your other fingers."

"Threatening a police officer. Hm. I wonder how the judge would take that," Manny said.

"Tell me!" I shouted.

"All right. Don't get hysterical. His name is Richard Henderson. He is from Los Angeles, and he's a CIA agent."

"He's a *what*?" I was shouting again. I couldn't believe what Manny had said, in spite of my promises.

"I told you you wouldn't believe it," said Manny smugly. "We checked out his story with the CIA, and he's the real thing."

"Let's just get this straight. Beard is a CIA agent? Well, he put on a mighty good show. I never would have guessed. What was he doing kidnapping me and hanging out with Kid?" I rubbed the back of my neck. It was getting tense.

"It seems that Kid is part of an international car theft ring. They steal luxury cars here in the States, truck them to Los Angeles, and then ship them to South America or Asia where they bring big bucks," explained Manny.

"So what does this have to do with Art?"

"Art just happened to be in the wrong place at the wrong time. You know that used furniture he bought for the office? Well, it used to belong to the car theft ring. They had it in the office of the business they used as a cover for their illegal activities. From what Henderson says, McIntire jumped the gun when they were moving the cover business to a different location and sold the furniture. Evidently, Art ended up with some of it. The only problem is that somewhere in that furniture is a flash drive with the names of contacts and drop-off places and schedules—enough to put several people away for years and years."

I was stunned. "You're kidding."

"Nope. I'm dead serious. Henderson says the CIA wants that drive, and they want it before the bigwigs in the car theft ring go into hiding. They want to try to simultaneously grab as many people in the ring as they can, so they need the drive to verify names and places. Do you have any idea where that drive could be?"

I shook my head, saying slowly, "So this doesn't have anything to do with stolen car parts, just stolen cars?"

Now it was Manny's turn to look surprised. "No, these guys only deal in big-time merchandise."

Still shaking my head, I said, "I don't know. Somehow in the back of my mind I associated them with stolen car parts." I shrugged. "But now that I think of it, they seemed too professional to just be dealing with stuff on a local level."

Manny nodded. "That brings me to something I'm supposed to ask you. We were wondering if you'd let us search for the drive in the furniture Art bought."

"Go ahead. They already tore apart the couch in my family room and didn't find anything." I paused, struck by a thought. Excitedly, I said, "They didn't even look at the one in Art's office though. I wonder if they weren't aware that Art bought two couches because he got such a good deal. The couch in Art's office has a washable throw cover on it because of all the dirt that gets tracked in, so it's possible they didn't realize the couches were from the same place."

"Do you mind if we go there right now?" asked Manny.

# Chapter Eleven

"HI, JERRY!" I CALLED TO Art's manager as Manny and I walked through the repair shop into the store and Art's office. "I need to get something from the office."

Jerry brought his head out from under the hood of a Lincoln Towncar to wave at us, but when he saw Manny, his expression changed and his hand came slowly down from the waving position. He looked surprised. I'd have to introduce Manny later when we weren't in such a hurry. Jerry was probably wondering what I was doing with a uniformed police officer, and I didn't want him to worry.

The office looked just as it had on Sunday night, except that the cardboard box lid Beard had taped over the little window was lying on top of the desk. I wondered what Jerry had thought of that. I removed a couple of pillows and pulled the cover off the couch. "There it is."

"Where do you think a flash drive would be in that thing?" Manny asked.

I stared at the couch, considering. Then I took a screwdriver off the desk and started prying the little upholstered panels off the front of the couch's arms. "Isabel Okawa gave us a lesson on upholstering furniture a couple of months ago. Quite frankly, there are lots of places a person could hide a little drive in a couch but only one I can think of where a drive would be hidden even from an upholsterer on a couch like this."

"You women learn the darndest things in Relief Society," Manny said, sitting down on the other end of the couch and watching me go to work as he stroked his broken finger.

"Hm," I grunted. "You should know. Hey. I'm not going to do all of the work. There are some scissors in the desk drawer. You can start on the other arm," I scolded him.

After we'd worked for a few minutes, I lifted the fabric from one arm; then I lifted the padding underneath. There, underneath the padding, was a little plastic bag stapled to the frame. I pulled out the staple with the screwdriver, holding the bag up for Manny to see.

"There. What'd I tell you?" I said triumphantly.

"Good work! Wait until Henderson sees this." Manny got up from where he'd been kneeling by the couch.

"Let's go show him." I was so excited I could hardly stand it. One of the things that had been worrying at me was the thought that "the boss" might send someone else when he didn't hear from Beard or Kid—or rather Henderson or McIntire—or the other two he'd sent. With the information Henderson thought was on that drive, they could possibly shut down the whole organization, and that would mean I wouldn't have to worry about them coming to get me or my family at some later date.

Manny slipped the panels under the couch cushions and started putting the couch cover back in place. "Let's put things back as much as we can so no one can tell what we were doing. We don't want there to be even the slightest chance that the members of the ring could be tipped off," said Manny as he patted the cover back into shape and replaced the pillows. "There, it looks just like we found it."

"Unless someone looks underneath, but there's no reason anyone would do that," I agreed, looking around the room to make sure we hadn't left anything out of place. It was just as messy as it had been on Sunday night. I resisted the urge to straighten everything up but gave into the urge to shove a file-cabinet drawer as far in as it would go (it never would go in all the way) and to put an empty potato chip bag in the waste basket. Jerry would at least expect me to do that much. I looked at the plastic bag in my hand. Someone might see it if I just carried it out. I took an empty manila file folder out of the drawer and put the plastic bag with flash drive inside. I also picked up some mail as camouflage. "OK. Let's go," I said.

"I can hardly wait to see Henderson's face when we show him what we found," said Manny as we walked out through the garage.

"Hey, Jane. How's it going?" asked Jerry.

I thought of telling him the whole story, but we were in a hurry to see Henderson. Jerry would get a good laugh out of it, but he'd probably be a little upset too. He was kind of like family, having pretty much taken over running the garage part of Art's Parts and even managing the store while Art had been in the hospital. I could imagine Jerry reacting protectively, much like Kyle had. So I just said, "Fine, Jerry. I do have something to tell you, but right now I have to get down to the police station."

Jerry blinked. "Police station?" His eyebrows came together in a little worried frown.

"I'll tell you about it later, OK?" I said, patting him on the arm as Manny and I left.

Manny drove as quickly to the station as he dared, which was pretty fast. I envied him the use of his squad car, since he was able to drive fast without worrying about getting a ticket.

Henderson's reaction was everything I could have hoped for. "Well, I'll be," he said holding the drive in his uninjured hand like it was gold. "How'd you find that?"

"She found it." Manny proudly patted me on the shoulder, and I tried not to wince. He was patting right where McIntire and Henderson had both squeezed so hard they'd left a big bruise.

Henderson turned to me, really looking at me for the first time since he'd quit acting like a kidnapper. He stared at my face. "Sorry about the black eye. You scared the living daylights out of me, grabbing for that phone. I could just see McIntire blowing you away or slitting your throat. He's quick to do either one. Rather a black eye than your life, I guess."

I felt faint. "I guess so," I echoed. "I'm sorry about your finger."

Henderson waved a newly bandaged hand. "You're a dangerous woman. Where'd you learn to do stuff like that?"

"From him." I pointed to Manny.

Manny just shrugged and held up his own bandaged hand.

Henderson just shook his head. He held up the drive. "I'll see if there's someplace around here to bring this up so I can get the information off it and e-mail it to headquarters. I guess this didn't turn out too badly after all. Thanks for your help." He held out his good hand to shake mine.

I shook his hand rather gingerly. It was still hard to think of him as anything but the man who had kidnapped me, although he had shaved off the beard and looked quite different. Hopefully I wouldn't have to see him again, unless it was in court.

"Will I have to go to court to testify?" I asked Manny as we went toward his desk.

Manny nodded. "Probably. Unless we can convince the judge to accept your statement as your testimony."

"Oh," I said. I wasn't looking forward to that, although now that I've done it, I realize it wasn't too bad. Boring, mostly.

Giving my statement wasn't too bad, either, especially since Manny shepherded me through the process. On the way home, I yawned mightily. "I could use a nap. I don't know why I'm so tired."

"Probably the release of all the stress you've been under," Manny said.

By the time we reached the house, I was fighting to keep my eyes open. My granddaughters were taking naps and so was Kyle, resting up after all the driving he'd done. Veronica looked like she wouldn't mind going to sleep either.

"Carline and Mary Ann have been calling every half hour since you left. I told them you'd call them when you got back," Veronica told me.

I yawned again. "Tell you what. Let's both take a nap. I'll call them when I wake up." I looked questioningly at the police officer reading a magazine on the couch. "Is that all right?"

He said, "Fine," and went back to reading his magazine.

When I woke up, the officer who'd been there during the day was gone, and Roberts and Greerson were back.

"We want to hear the whole story," Roberts announced when I walked into the family room. "We volunteered to take the swing shift at your house just so we could hear."

"Where are Kyle and Veronica and the girls?" I asked, sniffing at the smell of something wonderful cooking. The smell was coming from the crock pot. Veronica must have put dinner on, bless her. I wasn't looking forward to cooking anything at that moment.

"They took off to go house hunting," said Greerson.

"Oh," I said, disappointed that I couldn't see them right then. Those little girls needed to get to know their grandmother again. "Well, I'll call Carline and Mary Ann and see if they can come. I don't want to keep repeating everything over and over."

"Before you do that, you need to call that CIA agent, Henderson, down at the police station. He says he has some news for you," said Roberts, handing me a little slip of paper with the station phone number on it.

I hurried to the phone and dialed the number. When Henderson got on the line, he sounded like a new man. I hardly recognized his voice, he was so cheerful. "I just wanted to let you know everything went like clockwork. You can rest easy now. We've been watching the leaders of this gang for quite some time but didn't have the evidence we needed to grab them. The information on that drive was just what we needed to send in the troops. The gang members all behind bars except for a couple of small fries, and we're on their tails, so I don't think you need to worry about any repercussions."

"Really?" was all I could think of to say. I felt like crying again. My family was safe, really safe.

"Yep. My boss wants to congratulate you for your part in this," he said.

I wanted to say something about how involuntary my part in this had been and that it had been mostly his fault that I had been involved, but I restrained myself. "Thanks."

"Well, I've got to sign off now. I've got a plane to catch back to Los Angeles. The sergeant wants the officers at your house to call him soon. Good-bye and good luck." He hung up.

I told Roberts and Greerson that the crooks had been caught and that their sergeant wanted them to check in. When they called, they were told that they should head back to the station, since the danger to my family was past. They were disappointed, but I reminded them that they could read my statement and get the whole thing. To tell the truth, I was also a little disappointed I wouldn't be able to tell them my story, since the more I told it, the more amazing I realized it was. When they were gone, I called Carline and Mary Ann. I thought that at least my visiting teachers would want to hear it. But Mary Ann was at a little league game, and Carline's husband had invited one of his coworkers over for dinner, so we reluctantly decided that they would come over at about eight to hear everything.

Wandering back into the family room from the kitchen, I stopped by the couch and tried pushing the stuffing back inside the ripped upholstery, without much success. Too bad. Art would be sick when he saw the poor thing. It would have to be reupholstered, and it would be a headache, considering all the trouble we'd gone to getting just the right material to match the room. I wondered if our house insurance covered damage done by kidnappers. The insurance company probably wouldn't believe it, but the police would be able to verify my story. I also wondered if the upholsterer still had the same material handy.

The phone rang. It was a reporter from a local television station who had just gotten the story from the police about my kidnapping. When I realized it was the same station that

I had turned on to startle the kidnappers awake, I couldn't help chuckling. "Have I got a story for you," I told the bewildered reporter. "I'll give you a short statement now, but if you can wait until tomorrow, I'll tell you the whole thing. I just don't feel up to a lot of publicity today." She agreed to call back the next day.

After I hung up with her, the phone rang again. It was another reporter. This could get tiresome in a hurry. When I hung up with that reporter, I decided to let the answering machine screen calls. The phone rang again before I even got back into the family room. Sure enough, after Art's cheery message, I heard another reporter, this time from Denver. Word must be getting out. I supposed I'd have to talk to the press, but not today.

I sat down in the recliner then got up. The memory of being tied up in it was too strong. Sitting on the couch wasn't any better, and I definitely didn't want to sit at the kitchen table. Finally, I ended up in Art's desk chair. I ran my fingers over the pencils and paper clips and loose papers on Art's desk. That reminded me of the files Henderson had pulled out of Art's filing cabinet. Reaching over, I pulled open the cabinet drawer to see how much of a mess the files were. They were all back in the right places. At least Henderson was neat. I pulled out the file Henderson had looked through so painstakingly. As neat as he was, Henderson hadn't gotten everything into chronological order. I spread the receipts out on the desk and started putting them back the way they should have been, smiling a little as I thought of how Art's horrible handwriting had frustrated Henderson. A wave of longing for my husband washed over me. Manny had called the park rangers and asked them to be on the lookout for Art and the boys, so I expected the rest of my family to be home soon. Patting one of the receipts affectionately, I recognized it as the one even I hadn't been able to read. I squinted at the words on the receipt. The beginning letter was definitely a C. I laughed out loud when I realized that the receipt wasn't for clutches but for two couches. If Henderson had been able to read it, he would have probably ripped up the couch in Art's office and found the information himself. Who knows what would have happened then? I was just glad it was over.

I looked at the two receipts I'd thought were about stolen parts and frowned. It certainly looked like that's what Art had written on them. The other writing on the receipts wasn't Art's though. For the first time, I realized that the receipts weren't even the kind we used down at the shop. They were generic ones, the kind sold in any business supply store. Why did Art have those in his files?

"Mom?" called Kyle from the front door, and I heard the voices of little girls.

"In here," I called back. I got up to meet them, only to have two little bodies throw themselves at my knees. Cassidy, the littlest, toddled after them. "Hey, there! How are my favorite little girls in the whole wide world?" I exclaimed, plopping down on the couch, where I could hold all three of them.

Tessa pulled at some of the stuffing spilling out of the couch and held it up for me to see. "You sure don't take very good care of your furniture," she said gravely.

"Tessa!" exclaimed Veronica.

Just as gravely, I took the stuffing from Tessa and held it out for her to see. "There is a very good reason why the couch is in such bad shape. I'll tell you all about it over dinner. I'm starving, and your mother made something that smells very good."

# Chapter Twelve

"I'D HAVE DIED. I'D HAVE died right there," said Carline later that evening after I finished my story.

Mary Ann just shook her head. "How did you hold up? I'd have been a useless blob."

Shrugging, I said, "You'd be surprised at what you could do to protect your family. That's all I could think of. But I don't think I could have done it without a lot of help from above. My guardian angels must be worn out."

"Speaking of help, we *are* your visiting teachers. What can we do to help you?" asked Carline.

Mary Ann chimed in, "Yes, your van is out of commission for a few days, isn't it? Can we take you anywhere?"

"I need to go shopping, but Kyle or Veronica can probably drive me," I said.

"What about your van?" asked Carline. "You'll have to have the window replaced, but the brakes should be all right, shouldn't they? The rope tied to the brakes wouldn't have hurt them any, would it?"

Mary Ann leaned forward. "What I want to know is how Henderson and McIntire got the rope onto your brakes in the first place when they weren't anywhere near your house or the van until you got home from the Cub Scout dinner." She looked at Carline and me triumphantly, as if she had just come up with something brilliant.

I stared back at her. She was brilliant. I hadn't even thought about the rope on the brakes since I'd heard about the car theft ring leaders being caught by the CIA. Henderson hadn't ever mentioned the rope or the brakes. No one had. Why? Shaking my head, I said slowly, "I don't think Henderson or McIntire had anything to do with the rope on the brakes. The rope was tied in the wrong place to do any real damage. Whoever did it wasn't a pro like those two were."

Now Carline was excited. "Who else would have tied a rope to your brakes?"

I started to shake my head; then I went over to Art's filing cabinet and took out the two receipts for stolen car parts. Holding them up, I said, "Maybe the people who sold Art these stolen car parts are worried he'll turn them in to the police."

Carline squeaked, "Someone tried to sell Art hot car parts?" I could tell by the way she said it that she was proud that she knew the word *hot* meant stolen.

"Yes. It happens every once in a while. Art regularly checks serial numbers to make sure he doesn't buy *hot* parts, but sometimes they slip by." I emphasized the word *hot* for Carline's sake. "I'm afraid that once, instead of just taking the parts to the police, he threatened some kids and told them not to try to sell him stolen goods. It's possible they're the ones who put the rope on the brakes. What puzzles me is why the receipt is in this file at home instead of at Art's office. He usually keeps merchandise receipts in his office."

"Let's go to the office and see if there are any more receipts like this one," said Mary Ann.

"Why?" Carline asked, but I thought I knew where Mary Ann was going with the thought.

Mary Ann rolled her eyes. "Because there may be a clue on a receipt that will tell us who put the rope on the brakes. Jane, you were so afraid that *those* men would hurt your family, well, what about *these* guys? They tried to hurt your family already, didn't they? You don't want them to do it again, do you?"

I nodded. "You're right. Maybe we should go down there, but let's call Manny first. I'd feel better if he went with us." I went into the kitchen and called, but Manny was out finishing up his home teaching, since it was the next to the last night of the month. I asked Angela to see if Manny would meet us down at Art's office when he was through, and she said she would. I told Kyle and Veronica where we were going. Then we all piled into Carline's minivan.

"This is so exciting," said Carline, rather thoughtlessly, I thought.

"It's not so exciting when it's happening to you," I replied, rubbing my arms where the bruises were aching dully. Carline read mysteries like other people eat candy, so her grasp on reality wasn't totally there.

"Tell us again how you found the rope and about Art threatening those kids about the stolen car parts," said Mary Ann.

I went over the information one more time.

"So the kids who tried to sell Art the stolen goods told him they worked for a reputable wrecking yard. That's interesting," said Mary Ann.

"It is, isn't it?" Carline chimed in. "That means they knew which yards Art normally buys from." She was definitely pleased by having come up with that idea.

"Curiouser and curiouser," I said, quoting Lewis Caroll. "I think you two may have hit on something there."

"That's what visiting teachers are for," answered Mary Ann.

Hesitantly, I said, "I hate to think of the implications that possibility opens up. For instance, if that's the case, then someone who works for Art might be in on it." I frowned.

"You mean one of Art's employees? But who would do a thing like that?" asked Carline.

"Who has Art hired in the last year?" asked Mary Ann.

"He hired another mechanic to take the place of Evan's friend who went off to BYU, and he's hired a couple of counter clerks to help in the store. I just hate to think it could be someone Art trusts." It was bad enough being afraid of some gangsters, but at least they were strangers.

I guess that thought was depressing enough for all of us because we were quiet the rest of the way. I told Carline to pull around to the back and we'd go in through the garage. I didn't want anyone to know we were there in case whoever had tied on the rope could see. Once in the garage, we didn't turn on any lights, using Carline's flashlight to find our way around instead. Henderson had taught me a lot about being sneaky.

"Boy, this place is a mess!" exclaimed Carline as we walked through the garage.

"Shh!" shushed Mary Ann.

"Oh, there's nobody here," huffed Carline.

"Maybe not, but there was," I said.

I shined the flashlight around the garage. The bays were in good shape, like they were supposed to be, but it was a different story closer to the store. There were a couple of rows of shelves with used parts on them—Art liked to keep some in stock, but they were usually grimy, so he didn't want them in his store with the new boxed stuff. Usually the parts were kept neatly in their places on the shelves, but there were parts strewn all over now.

"What happened?" I was shocked at the mess. Art may not keep his office very neat, but his garage was his baby. He'd have a heart attack if he saw the place like this. So would Jerry. One reason Art liked Jerry was that the man felt the same way as Art about keeping the garage orderly.

"Somebody was either looking for something or took an unreasonable dislike to used car parts," said Mary Ann.

"But who?" Carline asked.

I waved the flashlight in the direction of the store. "Let's go look in the office for those receipts." Carline and Mary Ann followed me into the store and then into the office. I showed them how to tape the box lid over the office window and lay the couch pillows along the bottom to keep the light from being seen outside. They were impressed with my new expertise.

"Where does Art keep the receipts for merchandise?" asked Mary Ann, opening the top file-cabinet drawer and riffling through the files.

"Up there are the receipts for new parts. The bottom drawer is for used parts. The next to lower one is for receipts for the last couple of years in case we need them," I said, pulling out the drawer that never shut all the way and then shoving it in. It still didn't go in all the way.

"That thing sure is full. You guys do a lot of business," said Mary Ann.

"It's picked up some in the last few years, but that drawer is no more full than the others. It just won't shut all the way."

I pulled it out again to show her, only this time I pulled it out all the way. Sticking up just behind the end of the drawer was a file folder. "Hey! That's why it won't close. That file folder must have gotten stuck somehow." I pulled on the folder, but it didn't budge. Curious, I reached behind the drawer and felt around the edges of the file folder. It was taped to the drawer. I unstuck the tape, freeing the folder.

"What's inside?" Carline asked.

"I don't know," I said, opening the folder on my lap as I sat down on the couch. "Look! Receipts. Lots of them, and they look just like the ones Art had at home." I drew the two receipts that I'd found in the family room out of my pocket. Even the handwriting on them matched. The only difference between the ones I'd found earlier and the ones in the folder was what Art had written on them.

"Do you think those parts were stolen too?" Carline asked breathlessly.

"Why would they be hidden behind the drawer if they weren't?" Mary Ann reasoned. "Now, who has access to this office? Who could put them there?"

I wrinkled my forehead, trying to think. "The store clerks run in and out of here all day. Sometimes customers sit in here while they're waiting for their cars, but that's only if the couch out in the store is full, so it wouldn't be all that often. Sometimes the mechanics come in. It could be anyone." I shook my head in frustration.

"Well, we're not going to find out just sitting here. What should we do next?" asked Mary Ann.

"I guess we'd better turn this file over to the police and let them look up the serial numbers to see if they're really receipts for stolen parts." I shut the folder, standing up.

"Before we go, show us where you found that flash drive," said Carline.

"You and your mystery stories," chuckled Mary Ann.

"If you two will get off the couch, I'll show you," I said, taking off the couch cover when they stood. "Now, remember Isabel's lesson on reupholstering the furniture? Remember how she said we didn't need to mess with the padding if it was in good condition? Well, Henderson and McIntire had said something about how the furniture Art had bought had come from an office, so I thought it had probably been in pretty good condition, so whoever reupholstered it probably hadn't had to mess with the padding, especially on the arms. The couches had this little upholstered panel on the front that would be easy to pry off if someone wanted to get into the arm, which is also why I thought of looking on the arms. Sure enough, the drive was right there when we looked." I lifted the upholstery and the padding underneath to show them the staple holes in the wooden frame.

"Brilliant. Absolutely brilliant, my dear Holmes," Carline congratulated me.

"You are one smart cookie," said Mary Ann.

"Manny just tucked the little panels under the couch cushions and covered the couch when we left so no one would suspect we'd found the drive, but I think we probably ought to fix the couch, especially if we're dealing with someone dishonest who works here and has access to the office, don't you think?" I asked my visiting teachers, and they agreed.

"What we need is a hammer and a staple gun," Mary Ann said from where she was kneeling, trying to fit an upholstered panel back on one of the arms.

"I know where there's a hammer, and there may be a staple gun as well," I said, heading for the garage.

"Just call me Isabel Okawa," Carline was saying as I left.

I took the flashlight with me, slipping out of the office quickly to keep excess light to a minimum. If it had been smart to not turn on the lights when we'd come, it was doubly so now that we had that file. The hammers were on the wall on the far side of the garage, where Art kept all the tools neatly hanging on those pressed boards with the little holes in them. I knew right where they were, so I went there first.

Halfway across the dark garage, I realized how eerie it was. I was remembering how McIntire had shoved me along so I'd hit my foot on the car lift runner. The thought of that slimy creature made me shiver. My foot was still a little sore, if I touched it. I shivered again, looking around me. The wires and things hanging from the ceiling only added to the eeriness. They reminded me of snakes in the jungle just waiting to drop on unsuspecting victims. Nasty thought. My stomach started going all tense again, a feeling only too familiar after the last couple of days. I turned quickly to look for the staple gun and gasped as I nearly ran into an engine hanging from a winch ready to put into the car in the next bay. It was the Lincoln Towncar that Jerry had been working on earlier that day. Silly of me to frighten myself like that.

With the hammer in hand, I walked back through the garage, looking for the staple gun amid the power tools laid out on the bench, but I couldn't find one. The tiniest clank behind me made me whirl around, my ears straining to listen, my eyes staring into the dark shadows all around me. The sound had come from beyond the Towncar—between me and that nice, lighted office where Carline and Mary Ann were waiting for me. It suddenly seemed like a very bad idea for me to be all alone in the garage. I could feel my hands turn cold and sweaty. My heart was beating faster.

Cautiously, I stepped forward then listened. Nothing— except my heart thudding in my ears. I stepped forward again and again. I was right up to the front of the Towncar.

I tensed, ready to run. If there was anyone hiding behind that open hood, I wanted to be able to outrun them into the office. There was another clank, this time to my left. I turned just in time to see the hanging engine come swinging toward me, one chain flying free. Throwing myself to one side, I screamed as the heavy block of metal crashed into the raised hood of the Lincoln Towncar. I lay on the cold concrete for just a second in disbelief; then I heaved myself to my feet, screaming again. Strong fingers grabbed my arm, and a rough hand clamped over my mouth. Instinctively, I reached up, grabbed the little finger of the hand and yanked for all I was worth. Whoever was grabbing me yelled, letting go of me.

Lunging toward the store, I nearly ran into Mary Ann, couch cover in hand, just as she turned on the lights. She threw the cover over my attacker. He stumbled and then started to tear at the cover over his head, but I had grabbed one corner and Mary Ann grabbed the other, pulling him back against the wall. Screaming, Carline charged through the door and shoved a broom handle right into the man's stomach at a full run, doubling him over. Then, still screaming, she hit him over the head with it a couple of times, and he fell to the floor, face first. I jumped on top of him, and so did Mary Ann. After a moment's hesitation, so did Carline, still wailing on him with the broom handle for all she was worth. He struggled some, but Mary Ann and I managed to pull the cover around to his back and tie the corners together firmly in square knots my Cub Scouts would have been proud of, trussing him up tightly. With Carline and me still on his back, Mary Ann grabbed one of the nearby power tools, a staple gun, as luck would have it, and tied his ankles together with the cord. She grabbed another power tool, a drill this time, and pulled his hands around behind him. His hands were limp. He lay still. *At least if he was unconscious, his finger and his head weren't hurting*, I thought.

"You can stop hitting him now, Carline. I think you knocked him out," I said, thinking it was probably lucky for my attacker that the couch cover was still over his head. It had probably cushioned the blows.

She stopped hitting but continued crying. "Oh no! Do you think I killed him? I couldn't stand it if I killed him. I was just so scared, I kept hitting and hitting," she sobbed as Mary Ann lifted her up and held Carline in her arms. Mary Ann didn't look much better. She kept shaking her head in little jerks, looking down at the body at her feet, then closing her eyes. They reminded me of how I had felt when Henderson and McIntire had caught me. I wasn't feeling much better, but I guess I was getting used to this kind of thing because I kept fairly calm.

Rolling the man over and putting my hand on his chest, I said, "I don't think you killed him. He's still breathing, and his heart is beating. But we'd probably better get this off his head so he can breathe more easily." I pulled at the cloth until I uncovered his face. "Jerry!"

"Who?" Carline sniffed.

I was staring at the face in front of me in shock, feeling sick to my stomach. "It's Jerry. Art's manager!"

If this story had been a movie, the police officers, Manny, Art and the boys, and Kyle and Veronica and the girls would have come bursting into the garage at that moment, dragging Jerry off and comforting me and Carline and Mary Ann, but it didn't happen that way. My visiting teachers and I were left to figure out what to do next. The garage had never seemed so cold and greasy and dirty and just plain uninviting as it did while we stood around Jerry's unconscious body trying to decide what to do next.

Eventually, I had Mary Ann and Carline watch Jerry, who was beginning to stir, while I called the police station. The officer who answered the phone recognized my voice. She had been at the park and had helped capture Henderson and McIntire the night before, so she didn't question my request for some officers to come to Art's garage, for which I was grateful. I hadn't looked forward to trying to establish credibility with someone I didn't know.

"Was this guy one of the ones who slipped through the net when the feds were rounding up the car theft ring?" asked the officer.

"No. I think he's connected with something local, something totally different," I answered.

"Man, you sure do attract them, don't you," the officer said admiringly.

"Yeah," I agreed. "I sure do."

# Epilogue

I'VE BEEN WRITING THIS DURING the trial on the laptop computer Art bought me—another sop to his guilt over my having to face all those crooks on my own. I'll have to admit, Dr. Thornton was right about writing this all down. It has been therapeutic, and doing it during the trial brought back a lot of the little details that the lawyers really appreciated. This was Jerry's trial, not the gangsters'. That one is in Los Angeles in who knows how long. I have to go down there for that one too, but the trial date still hasn't been set. Those federal cases take forever.

Art and the boys showed up the next morning all worried because the park rangers hadn't gotten the story straight, and as far as Art knew, I was lying in the hospital recovering from things too terrible to imagine. He hadn't gone to Florissant at all but had just told our home teacher that as a possibility. Actually, he and the boys had hiked out where no one could find them, which is why it had taken the park rangers so long to get in touch with him.

When Art walked into our bedroom, I was lying there covered with little girls trying to tickle me awake. Needless to say, he was relieved, until he saw the dark bruises my nightie revealed. Then he gathered me up in his arms and held me just as I'd wished he would. Only, instead of saying comforting things, he muttered angrily about crooks and government officials under his breath, and his muscles felt hard and angry. I didn't quite catch what he said, but I was glad McIntire was behind bars and that Henderson had gone back to LA or Art might have been tempted to commit a federal offense himself. I was also glad Veronica had shooed her little girls out of the room, so they didn't hear their grandpa.

McIntire was extradited back to Los Angeles on murder charges and several other things. I think the Colorado authorities and the federal authorities are still working out where he will be tried and for what, since kidnapping is also a federal offense. His crimes were committed in several states, so it's going to take some unraveling.

The hardest part for Art, besides what happened to me, was realizing that Jerry, whom he'd really liked and trusted, had been conducting a stolen auto parts operation since he'd come to work at Art's Parts. He'd been the one who had loosened the chain on the engine block that had come crashing down on Art, just as he had tried to do to me. He'd actually hoped to kill Art, thinking it would be easier to pull the wool over my eyes, especially if he was left in charge of the garage and store.

Art's Parts had been the perfect front for Jerry. When I'd come with Carline and Mary Ann that night, we'd caught him in the act of trying to get rid of all the stolen parts he'd hidden among the legitimately purchased parts, which was the reason for the mess in the garage. My showing up with Manny, staying in the office all that time, and then emerging with a file folder in hand had spooked Jerry into trying to clear out any evidence that would link him to the stolen goods.

The kids who had tried to sell parts to Art had been new in the business and mistaken Art for Jerry, and yes, it had been some of those kids who tied the rope onto the van brakes. The judge in that case was just going to slap the boys on their wrists and let them go, but Art hired a lawyer to see they were put in some rehabilitation program, so that's where they are.

Me, I was just glad to have all the adventure over. I spent the rest of the week being pampered by a very contrite Art, who took me to places like the Broadmoor Hotel and Remington's for dinner. He even bought me several quarts of Häagen-Dazs ice cream and agreed to watch *A Guy Named Joe* with me, although he slept through most of it. The next Sunday being fast Sunday, I got up and bore my testimony about the truthfulness of Relief Society, the visiting teaching program, home teachers, and the power of prayer.

*NOTE: Like I said, Professor Mallory, if there is anything you want me to explain about bearing testimonies, Relief Society, or the visiting teaching program, I'd be happy to explain. If you'd like, you could come over for a family home evening and hear all about them. I'll even make chocolate chunk cookies for refreshments. McIntire really liked them, so I know they're good.*

# About the Author

DENE LOW HAS BEEN WRITING most of her life. Her first publication was a short story in the *Friend* magazine, called "The Comforter." She has heard from several people that it has been used at baptisms to explain the Holy Ghost, which is very gratifying to her. Since then she has been published in national and international magazines, newspapers and by national and regional publishers in fiction, poetry, nonfiction, and academic texts. Although she earns her keep by being a university professor, her first love is writing fiction. She lives in Utah with her husband and loves being visited by her children and grandchildren. When she is not teaching or writing or being otherwise sedentary, she loves to ride her motorcycle.